"The Mermaid's Song"
A Lesbian Romance

Jenny Bloom

© 2020
Jenny Bloom

This book is intended for Adults (ages 18+) only. The contents may be offensive to some readers. It may contain graphic language, explicit sexual content, and adult situations. May contain scenes of unprotected sex. Please do not read this book if you are offended by content as mentioned above or if you are under the age of 18. Please educate yourself on safe sex practices before making potentially life-changing decisions about sex in real life.

This story is a work of fiction. Names, characters, businesses, places, events and incidents are the products of the author's imagination or used in a fictitious manner & are not to be construed as real. Any resemblance to actual persons, living or dead, or actual events is purely coincidental. Products or brand names mentioned are trademarks of their respective holders or companies. The cover uses licensed images & are shown for illustrative purposes only. Any person(s) that may be depicted on the cover are simply models.

Edition v1.00 (2020.02.24)
www.JennyBloomAuthor.com

Special thanks to the following volunteer readers who helped with proofreading: Jenny, Naomi W., RB and those who assisted but wished to be anonymous. Thank you so much for your support.

Chapter One

It wasn't often I decided to take a bath at 10 o'clock in the morning or did so in my swimsuit. But this was for training purposes, meaning I couldn't get distracted by the ideas of what bath time typically meant. Low lights, scented candles, bubbles that cascaded off the rim while satin-smooth legs just barely poked out; I had to resist the urge to simply strip down and let all my worldly worries melt away.

Yes, today was the day that I, Rashmi Machelle, beat my personal record for holding my breath.

So, I lie there in lukewarm water, my ugliest one-piece suit covering what naughty bits bubbles usually would. My hands remained pressed against the sides of the tub, making sure no part of my face breached for air. It had to have been over two minutes at this point--maybe three, if I was lucky--and already I could feel my lungs numbing from carbon dioxide build-up. Every forum I read attested to this being the hardest part, so, I had to assume it was smooth sailing from here. Just had to let my mind wander away from the desperate need to inhale. Stay relaxed, stay determined, and—

"Rrooowarh!"

Sixteen tons of force slammed against my stomach as I let out a gurgling gasp. A flourish of bubbles escaped my lips, forcing me to breech the surface and gasp for air. My arms immediately wrapped around the perpetrator currently huddled on my stomach; a sopping-wet Maine Coon still hissing and sputtering at the edge of my tub. He immediately curled up against my chest, myself standing up to see what had freaked him out so much. My face deadpanned at the sight of a little, Siamese kitten, attempting to lift his front paws over the tub so he could join us. "Really, Ferguson?"

He responded with a desperate mewl.

I let out a sigh, gently pushing him away with my foot while stepping out of the tub. "Ferg, honey, this really isn't the way you make friends with Ralsy."

Ralsy let out a wet hiss in my arms, staring daggers at the kitten currently looping around my legs.

"Don't you start!" I turned the Maine Coon around so we were eye-to-eye. "You're supposed to be the alpha of the house. Maybe act like it and Ferguson won't literally run you ragged."

Ralsy just glared at me, tail flickering, obviously irritated.

"God, you're such a baby." I went to put him on the floor, only to pull him right back up as Ferguson made a jump for him. "Ferg, stop! I seriously can't hold him all day."

Ferguson simply meowed, circling like a shark who just spotted a baby seal. Ralsy's tail twitched nervously, ears flat while another hiss slipped out. All I could do was sigh and carefully navigate around the kitten (who seemed determined to slip under my feet at every opportunity).

Finally, I managed to push myself out of the bathroom, Ferguson skittering across my bedroom's carpeted floor as I went for my bed. There were plenty of high-up places my kitten couldn't reach yet--a wood dresser near my window, a closet vanity, a number of shelves filled with knick-knacks related to the ocean-- so I made my choice and carefully plopped Ralsy onto a bookshelf crammed with cat toys, beds, and other feline paraphernalia. He seemed satisfied with the choice, pawing over to the middle of the shelf while beginning to lick himself clean. Ferguson, meanwhile, let out a piteous mewl, upset that his prey was out of reach.

"Here, buddy." I snagged a plush burrito off the shelf and tossed it in his general direction. Ferguson took off like a rocket, tackling the toy to the ground as his back legs began to playfully rabbit-kick it. Ralsy simply eyed the toy for a moment before going back to his grooming. With the conflict resolved, I decided to look over myself, not at all surprised to find long strands of cat hair covering every inch of me. Three, long gash marks had clawed their way through my suit, causing the skin underneath to become red and irritated. Another sigh slipped out as I began to pull it off. "You're lucky this isn't my work suit, Ralsy."

The Maine Coon simply flicked his tail as I started back to the bathroom, making sure to close the door completely this time.

Now it was just me and my naked self, carefully inspecting the scratches in the mirror. My suit took most of the cat hair with it, but there were still some strands here and there, especially along my shoulders. I couldn't help but smile, rubbing a hand on top of my shaven head while reminiscing. How long had it been since my own hair was long enough to touch my shoulders?

Suddenly, my phone buzzed on the bathroom countertop. In all the cat chaos, I'd completely forgotten about it and the timer I'd set. Quickly, I scooped it up in my hands, thumb pushing for the home button as I stopped the clock app. Six minutes, forty-two seconds. With no way to tell how much of that was dedicated to breaking up the brawl.

"Suppose I could always go again." The idea lingered for only a few more seconds before I flipped to my calendar, still hovering at the top of the screen. There had been some reason it'd gone off, but for the life of me, I couldn't remember anything that was going on today.

Until I read the header.

"The photoshoot is today?!" I nearly lost grip on my phone as I sprinted back out the door, flying around the room as a naked blur. Some instinctual part of me managed to pull my curtains shut as I scrambled to get dressed, grabbing a pair of rumpled shorts near my laundry hamper while pulling a tank top off its hanger. "Jesus, I thought that was next week!" I immediately went for my swim bag next (Thank God I'd packed it days before) and jammed my feet into a pair of tennis shoes before running out of my bedroom. Ferguson was hot on my tail, darting after my untied shoelaces while I ran across my apartment living room. "No, sweetie, you stay here," My hand remained tight around my front door, foot carefully pushing the energetic kitten away. "I really don't have time to chase you around the third floor."

He let out a disappointed whine, like that was the highlight of his day.

"I'll be back later." Quickly, the front door opened as I slid out and slammed it shut, making sure Ferguson's head hadn't managed to squeeze out. After a few seconds, his claws began scraping against the door, another chorus of yowls slipping out. Part of me so desperately wanted to open the door and let him come with me, but then, in the next instance, I heard a loud thumping around in the living room, grabbing Ferguson's attention. His little paws darted away, and once more, the telltale sounds of him and Ralsy 'play' wrestling began.

"I'll buy you some chicken treats when I'm done." I promised the Maine Coon as I jogged to the stairs. Honestly, that cat deserved a lifetime of treats for all the trouble he's put himself through.

It's hard explaining to folks that my professional line of work is being a mermaid. I get the looks, the shaking of heads, the thought that crosses everyone's mind when I tell them.

'How the hell could you survive on such a stupid idea?'

Turns out, I'm not the only one in the world with such outrageous dreams.

Back in my hospital days, I'd spend hours searching the web on the topic, finding forum after forum of men and women alike who'd make real money by dressing up as a half-fish person. There were how-to videos on swimming realistically, entire companies dedicated to crafting the perfect monofin, a fin shaped like a mermaid's tail, and creating mermaid "suits" that were both comfortable and realistic. It started out as a pipe dream, something to keep my focus away from IV tubes and the generally grim prognosis one gets from having cancer.

My parents fully encouraged it, having been told by doctors and therapists alike that swimming was actually a great way for cancer survivors to get back in shape. Plus, having something else to focus on helped with the emotional side of recovery. They brought me books and movies all about the 'mermaid culture', evolving from cartoony and Crayola pictures with the 'happily ever after' endings to those cheesy Hallmark movies involving some mermaid-y element.

Once my days in white rooms ended, I was fully convinced; people could be a mermaid professionally and still make enough to survive, even thrive.

Mom and Dad, however, seem to think otherwise.

I can't entirely blame them. They had to pay a lot to make sure I didn't just up and die on them. There's a lot of looming debt that needs to be paid off, and really, they thought all of this would fade once I was out in the world. But if I learned anything during my hospital years, it's that life doesn't really care what you do. Eventually, everyone bites it, some sooner than others. I just got lucky. And I wasn't going to waste it.

I would, however, just barely make it on time.

Between my bike's chain popping off, a number of drivers who insisted the biker's lane was for their use, and somehow hitting every red light up the block, I'd managed to turn the corner for "Sammy's Swimtime" just as a van pulled up to the curb. A pair of employees were unloading what looked to be camera equipment from the back, midday sun catching off the reflective, black exterior on the side. They were followed closely behind by who I could only guess was the photographer himself—Ira LeBeau, the supposed wizard of fantasy photography. I wasn't entirely sure what to expect; over email, the guy sounded incredibly put-together, possibly leagues older than myself. He had that haughty air to him when he wrote emails back to me, like he'd been photographing celebrities all his life and was simply humbling himself to take my request.

The guy looked to be in his mid-twenties, with scruffy-black hair and red lumberjack shirt half-tucked into a pair of skinny jeans. He made it halfway across before noticing me, doing a full 180 turn as a frown crossed his face. "You seriously just got here, lady?"

"So did you," I pointed out. "And the name's Rashmi, not 'lady'."

Ira waved a hand, as if my name was too much for him to remember. "It's your money we're wasting, not mine. If you'd gotten here earlier, we could've started the shoot right away." He turned on his heel and started toward the building, myself hopping off and pushing my bike beside him. I figured if I was still riding, there wouldn't be any reason not to run him over. "Now we gotta wait for you to get changed."

"It's not that hard to put on a suit." I said. "Don't you have a ton of props to set up in the water?"

Ira shook his head. "Most of its photoshopped in. We just need a few things for you to interact with." He pushed past me and went through the doors, leaving me outside, alone, to quickly chain up my bike. I couldn't fathom how he'd gotten so many recommendations; his pictures weren't anything *special*, and that attitude alone should turn folks away.

Before heading in, I slipped out my phone and thumbed through his gallery I'd saved weeks ago. Dozens of men and women alike were perfectly placed in his fantasy scape, some dressed as Tolkienesque elves hiding in the forest brush while others posed gracefully next to bridges as fluttering fairies. The shots were gorgeous—professional enough to be featured in magazines—and all I could do was bite my lip.

Those pictures were *absolutely* worth his shitty attitude.

"You headed in?" The door swung toward me, a, 'Help Wanted' ad nearly crashing into my face as one of the employees of the pool stood waiting. Perfect brown eyes, curls of red hair slipping out from her updo; she was a specimen to be sure. I nodded dumbly, quickly shoving my phone in my shorts liner before shuffling in. She tilted her head at me, smiling awkwardly with a wave as the door shut behind her. I could only lament at the lost opportunity, rest a hand at my face still flushed with heat. 'Just go back really quick,' I thought to myself. 'Say your name, ask for a number, do anything but walk away!'

I walked straight into the changing room, defeat heavy on my shoulders. The rejection was quickly shaken off; I had to focus on the task at hand. It didn't take long to strip out of my shorts and tank top and put on my suit. It was just a drawstring two-piece, the top printed to look like a pair of soft-pink shells. A perfect contrast to my darker skin-tone, though now the scratches were on full-display. Maybe it could be worked into my backstory; a fight against a shark, or maybe a deep exploration surrounded by jagged scenery. Regardless, it was there; I had to make it work.

The rest of the outfit would have to be put on at the pool itself, which meant all that was left was the wig. I'd carefully set it on my head, adhesive applied ahead of time so I wouldn't have to try and wrestle it on. It was the longest wig I owned, a darker shade of pink in comparison to my suit and wound up with bits of netting and sparkling (fake) pearls. Curled strands tumbled over my shoulders, lightly brushing against my back while I found myself staring into the room's mirror. It was a sight I still wasn't used to.

Someone rapped on the door. "You ready in there? We got the scene all set?"

I managed a quick, "Yup!" before applying a quick layer of waterproof mascara and lipstick. There wasn't any time for eyeshadow, but it was like Ira said; everything was gonna be photoshopped anyway. I made a face in the mirror, smiled, and headed out the dressing room's door, monofin in one hand and mermaid suit in the other.

Chapter Two

It frustrated me to no end that I wasn't totally confident in my scaly alter-ego just yet. Once I made it to the pool, it was all eyes on me and my supplies in-hand. Ira was in a wetsuit, flippers impatiently flopping on the tile as he watched me make my way to the edge. The familiar smell of chlorine quickly filled my nose, a sort of reassurance that I was in my element now and no one could take that away. Without even glancing his way, I sat myself down and began working my monofin into my suit, careful to not tear at the seams. It was a delicate process, making sure the fin was secured in the suit in its entirety before I could slide it up my legs. Scales shimmered against the overhead lights as I pulled it past my tights, the band snug and secure around my waist. Like that, I was someone--something else--entirely. It didn't matter what anyone else thought, how rude the photographer had been, or how I'd totally wasted an opportunity to ask a cute girl now. This moment was all about me.

I slipped into the water feet first, careful not to scrape my fin against the side of the pool. The cuts on my stomach stung a bit as I submerged, reminding me how I'd have ugly gashes in my first, professionally taken pictures. I was prepared for a temperature shock, but the warmer was warmer than I first anticipated. The image of small children and older folk using this as their personal bathroom was quickly pushed from my mind as I ran my usual tests, swimming around a bit to get used to one fin instead of two legs. I even forced my eyes open (would need to for the shoot, anyway), and was pleasantly surprised to find them not burn the slightest. My head surfaced soon afterward; curiosity apparent on my face.

"You never been in a saltwater pool?" Ira asked. "It's what I do all my underwater shoots in, if I can help it."

Saltwater. I'd only caught a brief glance of the word on the official "Sammy Swimtime" website, but I didn't think *this* was what it meant. Being able to open your eyes with ease was a Godsend; I could count on both hands the number of eyedrops I'd spent at my local pool.

"So? Are we ready to go?" Ira's legs were already in the water, oxygen mask hanging limply against his shoulders. I flashed him a thumbs-up, and without barely a splash, he sailed across the water and up to me. "I'm not particular when it comes to positions," He began. "Just try not to look like you're made of plastic."

All I could do was furrow my brow. What the hell was that supposed to mean?

"How long can you hold your breath?"

"Three minutes, give or take." Maybe more, if I hadn't been interrupted earlier today.

"I'll follow your lead, then." Ira started futzing with his camera lens, taking a moment to peer through both above and below the water. "Do whatever feels right once you're under. I'll pick from the best."

That was really all I was gonna get. I hid my annoyance with a deep-bellied gasp before dipping down. Arching my back, my fin splashed above the surface as I propelled toward the set-up, trying to 'not look like plastic'. I could feel his camera on my back, the occasional flash of light indicating that our session had officially begun. Before I could even reach the coral set-up, I made a dash back to the surface, sputtering for air. My stomach was in knots, a cold chill running down my spine.

'This is stupid. What am I doing?'

Ira was still below me, camera flashing incessantly. I wanted him to stop, to give me five so I could find my head again. But he wasn't going to stop, and I knew it. Much as he acted like he couldn't give a rat's ass about me; I was still a client. This was as much for him as it was for me.

With another deep breath, I was back under, the thought of him being more professional than me acting as my focal point. As gracefully as I could, I swam toward the pre-set coral reef, nothing more than a few fake-looking rocks covered in a myriad of sea life. Some part of me wanted to touch the grainer-looking coral, so I let myself go, exploring the craftsmanship of each piece. It really was impressive; someone had taken a lot of time to get the angles just right, the colors realistic enough to be mistaken as living. Just for fun, I grabbed a clam shell off the reef and opened it slowly, mouth gaping at the pearl inside. A few bubbles escaped my lips as the camera flashed more furiously; the photographer must've found a moment he really didn't want to miss. I finally felt at ease, letting my fin dance around the coral structures, having myself slide between the openings of rocks while glancing up at the surface. This was the right thing to do. This was it.

And that's when I heard it. A commotion just above the water. Someone was yelling, then another person joined in. Even my photographer's concentration was broken by the noise, only to be startled as a cascading curtain of bubbles burst through the water. A pair of feet started kicking clumsily, trying desperately to reach the bottom of the pool. I saw him start to drop his camera and swim forward, realizing seconds later why he'd let go of what was likely thousands of dollars' worth of equipment.

It was a little girl.

She was slowly sinking to the bottom of the pool, dressed in a bright blue one piece and a pair of loose shorts. A long mess of red curls splayed outward like octopi's legs and her hands kept pawing at the water, pulling herself farther and farther down. A brief flash went across her face when she saw me-- excitement, maybe--and she opened her mouth, a large collection of bubbles escaping as joy turned to panic.

My fin kicked out before I could think, knocking over rocks and coral bits as I propelled toward the girl. In seconds, I had my arms wrapped around her waist, her armpits acting as a catch so she wouldn't slide away. With one good kick, my head burst through the water, catching a quick breath before ducking back underneath, using whatever strength I had to keep the girl's head above the water. I was swimming somewhat blindly now, uncertain where the edge was but furiously kicking to reach it.

Finally, a pair of hands caught my shoulder before I slammed against the edge. Someone else's hands scooped the girl under the arms and pulled her out, finally giving me a chance to breach and gulp down a proper lungful of air. One of the photographer's lackeys reached to grab me, but I waved them away, kicking off my monofin and pulling myself out of the suit. Back with legs, I swung myself out of the pool and laid on the ground, still breathing heavily while the adrenaline wore off. Somehow, through it all, my wig managed to stay in place.

Of all things, that's what I decided to focus on first.

"Bernadette!" A panicked woman cried out as the pool doors flew open. There she was--the cute employee who'd held the door open from me--running across the tile and gathering the little girl up in her arms. She wasn't fazed at all by getting wet, only holding the girl--Bernadette--in her arms. "Oh my God, Bernie--what were you thinking?! You scared me half to death!"

"But, Mommy," Bernadette pointed to me, her bluish eyes shining once more with tangible excitement. "It's a mermaid! A real-life mermaid!"

I quickly slid my lower half back into the pool, giving an awkward wave to the pair as I did so. One of the other employees offered a towel to Mom and she gratefully accepted, quickly burrito-wrapping Bernadette up in it. Seconds later, a man came bursting through the doors, middle-aged and face wrought with panic.

"Anika!" He fell to his knees, hand reaching to settle on the mother's shoulder. "I'm so sorry, she just completely took off."

"Daddy said there was a mermaid in the pool." Bernadette beamed, wiggling out of her mother's arms as she went charging back to me. I pressed my body against the pool as the kid ran right over to me, grinning. "And there was, cause, you're here! I really like your hair; it's got pretty stuff in it."

"Th-Thank you?" It was all I could manage before her Mom--before Anika, came storming over. The man tried following, but she held up her hand. scowling. "Thanks for dropping her off."

"But, Anika—"

"I'll talk to you after the class."

Something stirred deep in the man that set me completely on edge. His posture straightened, a look of hostility glinting in his eyes. Then, he glanced around the pool, taking note of all the visible witnesses, before shoving his hands in his pockets and trailing out.

Without missing a beat, Anika's hand grabbed Bernadette's as she spun her around, both staring into the other's eyes. "Bernie, you really scared me." Her voice was soft, barely above a whisper. "Do we run away from Mommy or Daddy?"

Bernadette looked down, her toes curling against the wet tile. "No."

"Why not?"

Bernadette sniffled, rubbing her face with the towel. "Cause I can get hurt."

"That's right." Anika scooped the little girl up into her arms, giving her a tight, wet hug. "I know you wanted to see the mermaid, but you still have to stay safe, okay?"

Bernadette nodded, glancing back down at me. "Sorry, mermaid. I wasn't safe."

"Ah," I was still reeling over the fact that Anika was taken, but it was important to play the part I'd set up. "That's...um...I mean, your Mom is right. You don't have gills like me, so it's important you stay in the shallows until you can swim better."

Bernadette nodded again. "I take swimming class."

"Do you?" I asked, smiling. "That's, uh, that's good!"

"My Mommy is the teacher." She glanced at her mom, any trace of shame from her near-drowning experience gone.

"I bet she's a good teacher." I said this looking straight at Anika, who only smiled somewhat sheepishly. I was about to say more when Ira suddenly bubbled to the surface, camera in hand. He peeled off his face mask and goggles, eyeing the mother and daughter like someone who'd just seen a fifty on the sidewalk.

"Hey, you," he pointed to Anika. "You that kid's keeper?"

Anika nodded, obviously conflicted between being offended and confused. "Can I help you with something?"

Ira swam over to the edge, gently handing his camera off to one of his lackeys as he pulled up completely. "I've never taken shots like that before. You should see them—totally dynamic and in-the-moment--they're probably the most real pictures I've ever taken."

"Likely because the kid was *actually* drowning." I muttered under my breath.

He waved me away, focus completely on Anika now. "Look, I'm not just gonna throw the girl into the deep end, but we could move our set to the shallows. I want to take more pictures of her with my client."

Before Anika could verbally slap the photographer, Bernadette let out a squeal. "I wanna swim with the mermaid! Mommy, please? I promise I'll listen, and do everything they say, and I won't even ask for any dessert tonight!"

Her Mom looked incredibly unsure about the whole situation—overwhelmed, perhaps--so I suddenly chimed in. "You could swim with us, if that's more reassuring. I don't mind?"

That got the room's attention. Even Ira hadn't seemed to think that a possibility, but once it was out there, he was completely on-board. "Yeah, I like where this composition's going. A mother and daughter, interacting with a mermaid as lonely as the sea itself. That's pure poetry."

Though I wasn't a fan of my character's portrayal, Anika seemed less convinced. She glanced at the wall clock, then back at her daughter. "But, my classes,"

"All I need is a half-hour, tops." The photographer reassured. "Think of it as discounted advertising for this place and your class."

I had to snort at that. But this seemed to fully reassure Anika as she set Bernadette back on the ground. "All right, fine. But when my class gets here, all your stuff needs to be out of the pool."

"Yeah, whatever," Ira was already moving back to his equipment setup. We watched him for a moment, Anika and I, before exchanging the exact same look.

"He's...certainly something." Anika began.

"I put up with it because of his quality." I quickly explained. "He's got a really impressive gallery."

Anika's lips slightly pursed before she turned to Bernadette. "Okay, Bernie; Mommy's gotta get changed into her suit so we can both take pictures with the mermaid. What do you say to her?"

A stream of thank-yous left Bernadette's mouth as she skipped excitedly beside her Mom to the changing room. Anika glanced over her shoulder one more time and offered me a wave, which I mimicked.

"Thank you again," she called before disappearing behind the changing room door.

Everything suddenly felt light, like I was drifting in some in-between state of awake and asleep. She was absolutely perfect—but she was obviously married—but they didn't seem to get along—but I couldn't just cut in and--

"Hey, Rashmi!" Hearing Ira call my name snapped me immediately out of my daze. "Hurry up and fish out your suit! We've got less than thirty minutes to make something great!"

Something great...the sentence bounced around my head as I dipped back underwater to retrieve my gear. For once, I agreed with this asshole.

***

Swimming in the shallows was way harder than the deep end. I wouldn't call myself a klutz in my mermaid suit, but it took a lot of effort to turn sharply with a giant fin pulling against the water; something way easier to do with more depth to work with. Adding to that, I now had to worry about a small child with about as much grace as a newborn giraffe. I was on pins and needles the entire time, trying desperately to not smack Bernadette in the face. Anika seemed to have her mostly under control, keeping Bernadette toward the far shallows and having her sit on the stairs when the photographer wanted anything deeper done.

Even with my sight blurred underwater, it was hard to miss how much Anika was secretly enjoying

21

this. She seemed like a natural, maneuvering through the water like she herself was made of liquid. We did a few poses swimming side-by-side, a few sitting on the steps with Bernadette excitedly holding one of the starfish props, and even one with me swimming up from the deep end, reaching out to Anika in the shallows while her arm remained firm around Bernadette.

"All right, that's enough." She walked Bernadette to the stairs, reaching for her towel set just off to the side. "I've got about twelve more kids coming in less than ten minutes, so it's time for you to go."

Ira nodded; his eyes were completely glued to camera while he flipped through his work. "Don't call me. I'll call you."

I couldn't help but frown as I watched his lackeys start to pack everything up. Was that meant to be said toward me, or for Anika? How long was this guy going to take to edit some pictures?

Anika cleared her throat, pulling my head toward her. "That was...certainly an experience. Thank you for letting Bernie do that with you. And for," she waved a hand, obviously still a little shook up about her daughter nearly drowning earlier.

I waved my hand, a sheepish smile spreading across my face. "No, it was nothing! If anything, you helped me. This'll really help kickstart my career."

"Oh! Are you a model, then?" Anika asked.

"Of sorts." I gestured to my tail, lifting it slightly out of the water. "I'm working to become a professional mermaid."

"Oh." Anika's expression was one I'd seen before—on my parent's face, to potential clients—it was nothing new to me.

Bernadette then came scurrying to the steps, a mermaid-printed towel wrapped around her petite frame. "Miss Mermaid! You gotta stay for swimming class! I wanna show all my friends that you're here!"

"Bernie," Anika began. "I'm sure she, ah," she paused, suddenly red in the face. "Oh, gosh, I never even asked you for your name."

I pulled my hand out from underwater to shake with. "The name's Rashmi. Rashmi...Pearlglade."

One of Anika's eyebrows rose, but Bernadette was completely into it. "Ooh! That's such a pretty name!"

"It certainly is...something." Anika smiled awkwardly. "But Rashmi might be tired from all that swimming. She could be ready to go home."

"How's she gonna get there?" Bernadette asked. "Mermaids can't drive cars."

"Oh! Um, see, I'm only a mermaid when I'm in the water." I said. "I get legs once I dry off." Good God, the web of lies only grew more and more tangled. But every mermaid needed a good story, right?

"Don't dry off, then!" Bernadette threw her towel onto the ground and stumbled down the stairs; lucky I caught her before she splashed back into the shallows. "Stay a mermaid! I wanna show Bethany, and Amanda, and Lexi! They said mermaids are made up, and I'm a big liar." Her lower lip stuck out in a pout, eyes wide and shimmering. "Pleeeeease?"

"Bernadette, really," Anika sighed, setting her own towel down as she waded down the stairs. "You can't force a stranger to do whatever you want. That's not nice. Rashmi might have more to do today."

I really didn't. This was as exciting as my day was going to get. Plus, I hadn't really gotten a chance to just talk with Anika. Ira made sure every second was spent barking orders and sticking our heads underwater. This was a good chance to really scope out my chances with her, as dirty as that made me feel. "My schedule's actually pretty open." I said. "I wouldn't mind hanging around, as long as you're okay with it."

"Well," Anika's brow began to furrow. "I mean, if you're interested, my swimming aid had to go on maternity leave recently. If you're looking to make a few extra bucks, I could probably persuade my boss to give you what he usually gives her."

It took me a second to process her proposal. I could feel my eyes begin to squint, a dark scowl etching across my face. "Do you think I need the cash or something?"

Anika looked taken aback. "Oh, no, not at all! I just meant—you had mentioned this 'mermaid' thing was your main livelihood. I can't imagine you make..." She must've realized how insulting that sounded, because the rest of her sentence quickly died off.

"You know," I hefted myself out of the water, tail splashing as droplets splattered against Anika's face. "I've actually got a few other things to do today. Maybe some other time."

The wind was completely knocked out of Bernadette. Her face began to scrunch up, eyes watering with tears. "Nooo, you gotta stay. I wanna show my friends!"

"It—It's her choice, Bernie." Gently, Anika gathered her daughter up into her arms and stood on the pool's top step, still grimacing at her choice of phrasing. "It was nice meeting you, Rashmi. I, uh, hope we see you again."

"Yeah." I watched as the pair started toward the door, likely to greet whichever parents would come in first. Bernadette turned her body around, her head poking over her Mom's shoulder as she gave me a tearful wave. I gave one back, a squirm of guilt tying a knot in my stomach before I shoved it away. "Screw that." Once the door to the pool closed and I knew I was alone, I quickly stripped my suit away and pulled my feet free of the monofin. Anika's proposal kept tumbling around my head, my face hot and bothered as it repeated. Like I needed someone's pity money; I was perfectly fine-off as it was.

"I get to do what I want to do." Grabbing my towel, I slipped quickly into the changing room, not wanting to stop and talk to a bunch of little kids or—God forbid—trying to face Anika again.

Chapter Three

In hindsight, going after her in the first place was doomed from the start. I should've just taken the loss when I didn't say hi at the front door of Sammy's, but it was pretty obvious she was already spoken for. Bernadette even called him, 'Daddy', which should've been the biggest red flag to me. Lost cause ahead, steer clear so the rest of your day wasn't fucked. But I had been suckered into that cute, freckled face, and now I was paying the price. Which, according to the register, was $4.89.

"Oof." The guy behind the countertop looked over my creation--a coffee-almond ice cream drowning in chocolate syrup and stacked high with an assortment of chocolate candy bar chunks. "Who pissed in your pool today, Rashmi?"

"It's your fault for pricing by weight, Hank." I handed him a five, my tongue partially stuck out. It was hard to stay somber when he became part of the conversation. "I'm liable to get fat because of you."

"Not a chance." Hank quickly doled out the change, dropping it into tips before I could get the opportunity. "You likely burn enough calories for all the customers in here." He waved a hand around the ice-cream parlor, a dramatic smile gracing his clean-shaven face.

Hank was a fellow hospital resident, having spent almost as much time as I did back in the day. I'd met him during my first round of chemo treatments; we sat on nearby chairs, himself a gaunt, pale-faced individual who somehow still looked happy to be there. We'd gotten around to small talk, which eventually devolved into an hour-long debate between using classic rye or marbled when it came to making a

Rueben sandwich. Hank was a talker, to be certain, but he always seemed to have just the right thing to say when needed. A flair for the dramatic, a showman till the end; he'd been the only one I'd kept in contact once my hospital days were done and over with.

"Seriously, though," Hank's hands rested under his chin, batting those big, blue, manipulative beauties at me. "What's going on? You're way too in your head today. Did the photo shoot *not* pan out?"

"You would know my own schedule better than me." I said.

One of his hands covered his mouth. "You did *not* forget. Rashmi, this guy's a legend! You know how many small-timers Ira's put on the map with his pics? The only reason he gave me the time of day was cause he owed me a favor back from high school."

"A favor you refuse to tell me the specifics of." I pointed out. "Or, anything of, really."

Hank just shrugged nonchalantly.

I let out an exaggerated sigh, slumping against the display case while I reached on top for a spoon. "No, I made it to the shoot. Ira seemed really excited for whatever pictures he got, but," Another sigh as I stirred my ice cream concoction. "There may have been a slight distraction."

Hank smirked, holding up his hands. "Scale of one to ten?"

The back of my head thumped against the display glass. "Nine."

"Holy shit." Hank laughed, the sympathy clear on his face. "Rashmi, nooo."

"She was a redhead with *brown eyes*, Hank!" I moaned. "And that body in her swimsuit; she might as well have speared me through the heart."

"Was that a purposeful fish pun? Hank glanced over at my cup, "Girl, your $4.89 is becoming soup."

I spooned a few bites into my mouth, shuddering as the cold sensation ran down my throat and sent a chill down my spine. Dark, bitter, and dripping with chocolate. "She even had a kid, Hank!"

"She did *not*."

I nodded, wiping the corner of my mouth with the side of my hand. "Oh, the cutest little thing, though. Totally thought I was a real mermaid."

"Uh-huh." Hank's attention was suddenly on the parlor's entrance, not that I noticed.

"I mean, that's usually a deal-breaker in my book," I popped a piece of chocolate bar into my mouth, chewing it thoughtfully. "But this kid didn't drive me absolutely crazy."

"Right." Hank straightened, a weird look on his face. "Uh, what's she look like? The nine's kid, I mean."

"Looks just like Mom. Red hair, freckles, big ol' eyes." I tipped the ice cream cup to my lips, slurping the last bits up with my tongue as the parlor door's bell chimed. "But it was totally a lost cause. I'm pretty sure she's married or got a boyfriend. That should've been the point I stopped, but I just couldn't—"

Hank suddenly held me by the shoulders, one hand tipping my bowl down as I nearly snorted out my ice cream. As the ice cream parlor door swung shut, there stood Bernadette, changed out of her swimsuit and wet hair pulled back into a high ponytail. She was holding that same guy's hand, the one who had dropped her off at the pool and gotten scolded by Anika. He looked suspicious as hell, glancing in every direction but at Bernadette herself, a face pale and sweating bullets.

"Just curious," Hank's voice was barely above a whisper, still staring at the man with Bernadette. "Did the supposed love-interest look something like that?"

I nodded, trying to turn my back to them as casually as I could. My stomach was in knots and not just because I didn't really want Bernadette to recognize me. "Hank, Anika was really cold toward that guy."

"'Anika'?"

"The nine, Hank."

He nodded, attention flickering between me and the pair.

"I mean, I don't know the guy," I continued softly. "Literally just have that first interaction to go off. Maybe he's just having an off-day?" I laughed nervously, trying to push away the nervous squirm in my stomach. "It'd be pretty *judgey* to just make assumptions, right? Hank?"

He didn't respond. Instead, Hank ducked underneath the countertop, producing a pinstripe apron in his hand. The parlor's logo was sewn into the middle pockets, accompanied by what looked to be a flavor menu. "Here." He slid it toward me, eyes suddenly cold, calculative. "Come back here for a second."

"What? Why?" I asked.

He raised his brows at me, a frown on his face. "Just for a bit. I wanna see something."

"You offering me a part-time position or something?" My laughter was cut short when he remained silent, fixated on Bernadette and her 'Dad'. Without another word, I slipped the apron over my head and started toward the break in the counter, Hank, passing me by wordlessly. His body posture went from rigid to relaxed in seconds, a brightness in his voice that he didn't have seconds before.

"Hey, there! You two first-timers here?" he asked.

I shuffled to the cash register, still tying my apron strings while I watched the interaction. Bernadette was swinging her legs excitedly in her chair, an ear-to-ear grin on her face as she nodded. "I never been here! But Daddy said we can get ice cream."

"Oh, that's great!" I watched as Hank looked toward the man, his expression innocent and genuine. "Your Dad is so nice to get you a treat."

Dad nodded, face still cold and clammy.

"I did real good at swimming today," Bernadette continued matter-of-factly. "And you gotta eat when you're all done, or your tummy'll hurt."

"Can't argue with that logic." Hank beamed. "Actually, kids under ten get a small cone for free. Did you know that?"

Bernadette let out a gasp. "I'm only seven years old!"

Hank's hands clapped against his face. "What? But you look so much older!"

Bernadette's grin was infectious; I couldn't help but smile, too. Even Dad wasn't immune to the cute display.

"We got a whole bunch of flavors to choose from," Hank passed Dad the menu. "So, if you find one you like, just come on up to the counter and pick what you want. We price by weight, too." He added with a wink back toward me. I just shot him a look, still smiling.

"Nothing for me." Dad handed the menu back just as quickly as he got it. "She'll get a small vanilla."

"But, I wanna pick." Bernadette said.

"We don't have a lot of time, Bernie." Dad insisted. "Just a vanilla, please."

"Would you like to try some samples, maybe?" Hank's businessman voice was in full swing now. "All our ice cream's ready to scoop out for our customers; vanilla actually takes longer to get, since it comes from a machine. And, boy," he added with a dramatic sigh. "That thing's sure been on the fritz, lately."

Now I was confused. This place didn't even have an ice-cream machine, so what the heck was Hank talking about?

"I think I've got your favorites pinned, little lady," Hank crouched down to Bernadette's level, hands on his knees. "So, if you want, you can come up to the display case and see if I'm right?"

"Just get her some damn ice cream!" I was certain Dad realized his voice was way too loud. The other patrons turned his way, one mom even covering her kid's ears and scowling at him. Dad sank into his chair, eyeing the exit as he waved to Bernadette. "Be quick, okay?"

Bernadette practically fell out of her chair as she scampered up to the counter. Hank nodded to Dad, his expression immediately changing to a scowl as he made his way back to me. That squirm in my stomach had turned into full-blown nausea; what did Hank know that I didn't?

"Mermaid-lady?" My attention was pulled to Bernadette, squinting at me with a frown on her face. "Is that you?"

I sheepishly smiled. "Hi, Bernadette."

"You work at an ice cream store?" Bernadette asked. "Is that why you couldn't stay swimming?" She tilted her head, pointing a finger at my shaven head. "Where's your hair? Does it go away when it dries, too?"

I should've been somewhat offended at that, but at this point in my life, Bernadette hadn't been the first child to ask that question. Maybe not specifically if it fell off when it dried, but, still. All I could do was nod.

"Oh! Do you know my co-worker?" Hank's voice was just loud enough that everyone, including Dad, could hear.

"Yeah!" Bernadette said. "She was the pretty mermaid at the pool today!"

The flash of recognition ran past Dad's face. In one swift motion, his chair was pushed in and the door was pulled open, the chiming of bells alerting Bernadette. She spun around on her heels, panic in her voice as she watched her Dad run out. "Daddy, wait! I didn't pick yet!" Bernadette made a mad dash for the door, only to be stopped by Hank's arms gently catching around her chest. "Daddy come back! I'm sorry! I'll pick faster!" Tears were well past the point of flowing down her face, her joyful mood quickly soured by loud sobs. Now people were getting up out of their chairs, a few glancing out the windows while some took a few steps outside, as if debating if they should run the guy down or not. Some even had their phones flipped out, likely dialing 9-1-1.

"It's okay, it's all right," Hank started to gesture to me, but I was already halfway over the countertop. Health code be damned; it wasn't like I actually worked here, anyway.

"Mommy!" Bernadette sobbed, throwing herself into my arms and quickly soaking my sleeves with tears and snot. "I want my Mommy!"

I felt my face flush, even though I knew full-well she wasn't referring to me as such. "It's okay, Bernadette. We're gonna call your Mommy to come get you." I tried to stand but found her arms around my like a vice. Luckily, she wasn't too heavy, so I could pick her up easily. "Listen, Bernie? While we wait for Mommy, I need some help with something."

Bernadette rubbed her eyes, nose still running, but attention on me.

"See, mermaids are very particular with ice cream flavors." I turned her toward the display case, doing my best to smile warmly. "I just can't choose. Can you help me pick one?"

"That's a great idea." Hank stepped back in, pointing behind the counter as he added, "Sample spoons are right there. I don't usually let kids in the display, but," He gave an over dramatic wink to Bernadette. "If it's to help my mermaid friend, I think I can make an exception.

A few hiccupping sobs escaped Bernadette, but she gave me a nod. We started toward the break in the counter (I didn't think it responsible to try and jump over with a kid in my arms), Hank returning to customers as everyone got their story straight.

Already, I could hear the telltale shrill of police cars, but for now, my focus was on one thing and one thing only. "So, what flavor should I try first, Bernadette? I'm pretty partial to blue myself."

Bernadette gave a shaky laugh. "B-Blue ain't a flavor."

"Sure it is!" I said. "What would you call it, then?"

"Blue Razzberry." Bernadette answered smartly. "Or, bubblegum."

"That's pink." I pointed out.

"It can be blue!" Bernadette said. "Bubblegum can be a lot of colors."

"Can it?" I shifted her onto my hip, my other hand reaching for the small sampler spoons.

"Sure can." Bernadette said. "It can be blue, and pink, and yellow," She continued listing off colors, having seemingly forgotten how her Dad had ditched her. I nodded intently, occasionally glancing at the front door as Hank waited for the police to arrive. Guess if a kid was gonna get abandoned, an ice-cream shop wasn't the worst place.

***

It didn't take long for Anika to come. She'd still been over at Sammy's Swimtime, blowing up Dad's phone with a hundred or so voicemails once she realized he'd absconded with Bernadette. The police took about a twenty-minute drive to go pick her up, leaving me and the kid just enough time to finish sampling every flavor the parlor had. Once Anika burst through the door, though, not even ice cream could distract Bernadette.

34

"Mommy!" With a spoon full of Rockin' Chocolate Fudge still in hand, Bernadette hopped down off the counter and ran head-first into her mother. Anika didn't seem to care at all that her nice, white blouse had just gotten smeared with chocolate; Bernadette was immediately lifted into her arms, sobbing tears of relief. The other customers looked equally relieved, reassuring Anika that her child had been perfectly safe, that some of them had gotten a good look at the guy, asking if she needed anything, anything at all.

"Water would be great." Anika said.

One particularly sharp-looking officer took it from there, gesturing to Hank as they helped other officers play crowd control. I immediately went for a cup under the counter but stopped as my fingers touched up against the plastic. I'd completely shot down her offer at, 'quick cash', so what would she think seeing me here?

"Hey, Rashmi?" Hank's voice broke through my doubtful haze. "Can you grab a cup of water?"

I straightened, wiggling the cup in my hand as Anika and I caught eyes. Her initial reaction was surprise, brows arched upward while her mouth shaped a little 'o'. It persisted as I filled up the cup and started over; all I could manage was an awkward smile.

"Hi, Rashmi!" Bernadette waved happily, spoon partially in her mouth as chocolate dribbled down her chin. "Mommy got to ride in a police car."

"Did she?" I set the cup down beside Anika, but her gaze remained fixed on me.

Bernadette nodded, clicking the plastic spoon around her teeth. "Yeah. Mommy doesn't have a car and Daddy drove me here." As if reliving the scene from earlier, Bernadette's shoulders began to shake, sniffles coming from her mouth.

"Oh, sweetheart," Anika pulled Bernadette into her lap, carefully removing the small, plastic choking hazard from her mouth. I held out my hand and she gratefully placed it in my palm. "You know Daddy loves you. He just makes...silly choices sometimes."

Bernadette just rested her head against her mom's chest, tears streaming down her face.

Resting a hand on her head, Anika glanced up at me. "This is twice you've kept my daughter safe today. I don't know how to thank you."

"O-oh!" Face red, I quickly pulled Hank to my side, who'd been previously in-conversation with a police officer. "I mean, it wasn't--my friend here was the one who did everything, honestly."

Hank put on a friendly smile, placing an arm around my shoulder so I couldn't wiggle away. "Your daughter was in great hands. She and Rashmi here made sure all the ice cream was good enough to serve."

"Oh, gosh," Anika went for her purse, still protectively holding Bernadette against her chest.

Hank waved a hand. "Hey, samples are free for a reason! Don't worry about it."

Anika let out a sigh, slumping against the chair like the weight of the world had just been lifted. "Thank you, really. It's been a crazy couple of weeks, and I just," She quickly wiped the corners of her eyes. Hank's elbow dug subtly into my ribs, forcing me to look down at a napkin he'd snagged earlier off the table. I grabbed it, offering it to Anika, and she took it gratefully.

"Mrs. Church?" The sharp-looking officer stepped forward, flipping through a few notes in his booklet. "Sorry--Ms. Jenner--we've taken statements from everyone in this parlor except for you. And…," He gestured to Bernadette, still half-sobbing against her mother's chest.

"Does it have to be now?" She asked. "If you call my lawyer, he can tell you everything about my ex."

Hank raised a brow toward me. I did my best to keep a straight face, but it was somewhat satisfying to hear she and him were split.

"If I may be frank," The officer got down on one knee, taking off his hat while running his hand through shortly cropped hair. "We're more interested in what your daughter has to say about this. What Mr. Church may have said to her, if he was planning to take her anywhere else; this sort of information is especially prevalent in your sort of case."

Anika's other hand wrapped around Bernadette's waist, pressing firmly against her back. "Does it matter? He broke our agreement; why can't you just arrest him?"

"It's not that easy. We can't just," The officer glanced around, briefly catching Hank and I still standing nearby. The look he gave was louder than any statement he could've made.

"Um, let us know if you need anything else." With that, Hank and I started toward the backroom, myself in a semi-choke hold while we walked.

***

37

I managed to break away just as the door to the outer seating area swung shut, feeling the indignation rising in my gut.

"Did you have to drag me out like that?" I hissed.

"Sorry, sorry," Hank looked positively giddy, unable to contain his excitement. "This is just-- Rashmi, I work a boring nine to five, and I just stopped a potential kidnapping!"

"Come on, it wasn't a—" I stopped, shaking my head at the very idea. I mean, it couldn't be considered 'kidnapping' if Bernadette was that guy-- Mr. Church's--daughter, right? "How'd you know something was up, anyway?"

Hank shrugged. "Just got a bad vibe, is all. You kinda pick up on stuff like that when your first job is at the sketchiest gas station in town." He was still smiling. "Did you see me, though? Cool as a cucumber the whole time; look at this!" He held out his hand to me, the fingers visibly shaking.

"Jesus, Hank." I sandwiched my hands around his, trying to be of some comfort. "Take a breath. You didn't talk down some mass shooter or something." He gave me a wide-eyed look and I let out a sigh. "It was pretty impressive, though. I honestly don't know if I could've done it."

Hank nodded, apparently satisfied with my praise. After a beat or two, he added, "So she's divorced."

My hands went back to my side. "Shut up, Hank."

"Oh, come on!" He followed me as I started wandering the back room, feigning interest in the complex machinery and tubes that ran to the multiple freezers. "You were gushing like a schoolgirl when you first came in. I'm not saying jump in bed with her,"

"Hank,"

"But she looks like she could use a shoulder to lean on." Hank turned me around, hands on my shoulders as he gave me a wink. "That's how it all starts, anyway."

"You're an awful person." I'd been thinking the same thing, but I wasn't about to admit it. I pushed him away, arms crossed over my chest. "Anika's obviously going through some rough shit. Why the hell would I want to get involved with that?"

"Cause you can relate?" Hank offered.

"I've never been married." I said.

"No," Hank began. "But you and I have both had the metaphorical rug pulled out from underneath us. We can sympathize."

"With a total stranger?" I asked.

"*We* were total strangers," Hank pointed out. "And look where we are now!"

My expression deadpanned.

"Look," Hank's tone turned uncharacteristically serious. "I barely get to see you as is, what with you so focused on kicking off your mermaid career. I'm not saying to stop, but I am saying it gets lonely in an apartment by yourself."

"I have cats," I murmured under my breath. "And forum friends." My arms were less crossed now and more hugging my waist. "Anika wouldn't want me, anyway. Remission doesn't mean, 'gone forever'."

Hank suddenly pulled me into a tight hug. I hadn't realized it, but now I was the one who'd started shaking. We stayed like that for a moment, not talking, not making a sound. Just taking in the comfort of having someone there. After a moment, we pulled away, Hank taking out another napkin from seemingly nowhere.

"Where the hell do you keep getting this?" I half-giggled, half-sobbed, taking it as I wiped my face. Then, I took a deep breath, staring at the door behind Hank. "Okay. But I'm just gonna talk with her. Bernadette might get upset if I just suddenly vanish, anyway."

Hank just grinned and patted me on the shoulder. I gave him a punch back before pushing past.

Chapter Four

As I stepped out from the back, there seemed to be less people in the parlor. The police had dispersed by now, having finished gathering whatever info they needed. Some of the customers had left as well, though some remained around Anika's table to keep her company. She looked completely done with it all, Bernadette half-asleep in her arms while she forced a grin to the surrounding people. I know they were just trying to help, but it was clear Anika wanted them to piss off. I wasn't really sure how to approach this; by all intent and purpose, I was just another pestering passerby. What difference would I make, anyway?

"Hi, Rashmi." Bernadette called out sleepily, giving me a lopsided wave.

"Hi, Bernadette." I started toward the table, taking a seat in one of the open chairs. Others must've caught on that I had the situation handled, because the once-larger crowd began to break off, some going back to their desserts while others left the store altogether. Bernadette's eyes were barely open, her head snuggled up into the crook of her mom's neck. "You look tired." I said.

"Mm." Bernadette mumbled.

Anika carefully shifted her daughter in her lap, glancing at her watch. I craned my neck behind me, catching a glimpse at the time on the wall; was it almost 5 o'clock already? Felt like the whole day had raced passed me. I was certain Anika felt the same.

"I don't work here, by the way." Not sure why those were the first words out of my mouth.

"Excuse me?" Anika asked.

"At this place," I quickly untied the apron and shrugged it off. "I don't work here. Hank—the guy you met earlier—he just gave it to me to pretend."

Anika looked confused.

"I just didn't want you thinking I was a hypocrite," I continued. "I wasn't *exactly* gracious toward your offer earlier. Of, um, being a swim coach."

"Oh." Anika shook her head, "No, that's—I didn't even think of that, honestly."

She was a pretty bad liar; her lower lip pulled in as she bit it, eyes briefly darting away from mine. I let it rest, though. No real reason to keep bringing it up.

"I'm sorry about that." And here I was, still bringing it up.

"Really, it's okay." Anika's hand gently rested on Bernadette's head, who was fully knocked-out at this point. "Honestly, I'm just grateful there's people like you in the world. Bernadette is just so trusting, and to think she almost..." Now the tears were more than visible. There was no number of blinks that could get rid of them. "Oh, gosh, sorry. This must be really weird to have a total stranger just, completely break down like this."

"No, it's fine!" I reassured. "Breakdowns are sneaky like that. Probably best to just let them have their moment."

Anika's giggle sent my heart a-flutter. "Well, I really appreciate all you've done for me, Rashmi. I'd hate to keep you, though," she glanced at her watch once more. "Bernie and I have another hour or so to wait for the next bus home. I'd hate to keep you here."

I was mentally kicking myself for not owning a car.

"Not to be totally nosy," Hank suddenly appeared at the table, grinning from ear to ear. "But where is it that you live? My shift doesn't end for a while, but I trust Rashmi here with my keys."

I shot Hank a wide-eyed look, but Anika spoke before I could. "Oh, no, I couldn't ask that. We live about a half-hour away by car; that's a long way to go, especially if you live in the opposite direction."

Hank shrugged, still grinning. "Well, maybe you two aren't in the opposite direction. Rashmi lives at Oak Flats; that apartment complex on Centerburg?"

Another look was shot at Hank. What the fuck—who was he to just hand out my address like that?!

Anika let out a small gasp, "Wait, really?"

Cat's out of the bag, now. "Uh, yeah. Do you live close by?" I asked.

"If the first floor is 'close by'," Anika began.

Now I let out a small gasp. There was no way.

"What a coincidence!" Hank laughed, pressing his Volkswagen keys into my hand. "Rashmi would have no problem taking you there, then."

"But, my bike—" I started.

"I'll lock it up in the store." Hank insisted. "Like I said, my shift isn't gonna end soon, so I'll just take a bus."

"Would you really mind?" Anika asked. "You've done so much already for me, but I'd really appreciate it."

I was honestly still reeling over the fact we were neighbors. She'd been two floors down this entire time? How had I never run into her? Was Fate just feeling extra frisky today? It took a second to realize everyone was still staring at me, waiting for a response. All I could muster was a nod.

"Great!" Hank slapped me on the back, semi-throwing me off my chair and up into a standing position. "Then that settles that. Call me if you need anything, all right, Rashmi?" He gave me a wink and another few pats on the back.

"Y-Yeah." I nodded again, glancing over my shoulder at Anika. "So, um…I don't think Hank owns any special car seats or anything for Bernadette." Kids needed stuff like that, right?

"She clearly has someone watching over her today," Anika began. "As long as you drive safe, she'll be all right."

Right. Okay. That wasn't really reassuring. "All right. Then…let's go home."

***

There was no way in hell I was telling Anika that it'd been a year since I last drove. The city was too crowded, too limited in parking; I could get anywhere I needed and save the environment by bike. Plus, whatever I had to bring with me usually fit in my bag (unless it was grocery day, but that's what a bus pass was for).

So, it was safe to say I was overly cautious while driving the pair home. Bernadette was completely sprawled out in the back, half-buckled in the middle by her mom so there were at least some safety elements. Anika, meanwhile, was up in the passenger seat, holding a vice-grip on the door's

44

handle while we slowly crept through traffic. I glanced over at her occasionally, wondering if I was really that bad of a driver.

Anika must have noticed, because she gave me a reassuring wave. "Oh, no, it's just me. I always feel better driving myself." She paused, adding hastily afterwards, "Not that I'm saying your skills aren't— you're doing great!" She must've been still hung up about that mermaid comment earlier. There was something endearing about the thought; I couldn't help but smile.

Approximately a half-an-hour later (give or take a few minutes thanks to idiot drivers and cheeky red lights), Oak Flats appeared just off to my left. It was weird pulling into the parking lot instead of going straight through the doors. I made sure to pick a spot completely void of cars, not really wanting to bang up any part of Hank's ride on accident. I turned the key, engine sputtering off, and we all sat there for a few moments, the events of the day really sinking in. I still couldn't believe it; I'd gone from hitting myself for not saying hi to Anika to having her sitting right across from me. My hopes had been dashed when Mr. Church came in, but reignited when the 'ex' had been put in front of his name. Was I still a horrible person for wanting to go out with her? After today, it was obvious she had so much going on in her life. Was another relationship what she really needed? Was she even *interested* in the same sex like that?

"Thanks again for the ride." Anika began.

"Oh!" I blinked, looking toward her with a smile and thumbs up. I had to stop getting so lost in my head. "Yeah, of course."

"It's been such a strange day," Anika leaned back in her seat, eyes closed, hands folded on her lap. "But I can't say it was all bad. I learned I have a great new neighbor just a few floors away."

She called me a "great neighbor." Was that like being friend zoned?

"Anyway," Anika glanced back at Bernadette, still out like a rock. "I suppose she'll want dinner once I wake her up, so I better get started. I must sound like a broken record, but, thank you for everything, Rashmi."

"We'll have to do this again sometime." The words were out of my mouth before I could stop them, so I quickly added, "I mean, minus the whole drowning and runaway ex thing."

Anika laughed—a tired, heavy sort of sound you make just before you break completely—and she unbuckled herself from the passenger side. Bernadette's eyes fluttered slightly, a big yawn escaping her lips as Anika opened the door. "Bernie, sweetie, it's time to wake up."

Bernadette let out a grunt, rolling over in her seat as the buckle caught against her chest.

Anika sighed, smiling softly while she undid the fastens. She scooped Bernadette up into her arms, careful not to hit her head—or her kid's—against the car's roof. "I'll...see you around, then, Rashmi."

"Yeah."

She stood there for a second, slightly bemused. I couldn't figure out what was so funny, until she added, "Are you gonna sit in the car for a while, then?"

"Oh!" Hastily, I sprang out from the driver's

side, nearly choking on my seat belt as I did so. "No, I—haha, no, I'm coming in." That smile nearly made me trip over my feet. I managed to get the door to close, locking the car with a click of the button. I wasn't *really* ready for this, but, in hindsight, we did both live in the same building. It would've looked weird if I'd just watched them walk in without another word, so, in a way, this was probably better. That didn't mean I was going to enjoy trying small talk.

Almost as if sensing that, Anika started things off. "So, being a mermaid, huh? You must really like them if your whole job's modeled off them."

This I could work with. "Uh, yeah! Really liked them when I was a kid, so, why not make money off it?"

"How'd you even think of it?" Anika asked. "I have to admit, it wouldn't be something my high school advisor would tell me about."

I grinned at just the thought. "It'd be pretty wild, yeah. But uh, no, I had a lot of time to think about what I wanted to do." I gave my head a pat, "When you're told you have cancer, you do a lot of thinking."

"Oh." Anika's eyes widened as she looked down at the asphalt. "I'm sorry—I mean, I thought—but I didn't really want to say."

"Hey, it's not a swear word or anything," I said reassuringly. "Just a part of me. Besides, it's in remission right now, so I just get to wear it like a badge."

Anika glanced up, awkwardly grinning. "I couldn't imagine someone actually making a badge like that."

"Don't doubt," I said, a note of seriousness in my voice. "People make all kinds of crazy stuff. I went to an art show where someone was selling homemade mugs with the word, 'Unt' written across."

"'Unt'?" Anika's brow rose slightly. "I mean, I suppose nonsensical words count for crazy."

"But picture what a cup looks like," I said. "And imagine the handle is the starting letter instead."

Anika's face went blank for a second, the gears in her mind visibly turning as she put two and two together. Then, suddenly, a snort flew out of her mouth, to which she quickly tried covering her mouth as a fit of giggles followed suit. "No—that's terrible!"

In truth, I was relieved. She had a kid, after all, so that story may have been too dirty. But, much to my delight. Anika seemed to appreciate the fine art of insulting mugs. We continued to chat about one obscurity to the next—our first high school jobs, eating entire packs of gum in one sitting, if turquoise belonged with the blues or greens—even after the front door to the lobby had been pushed open. My intentions aside, it was nice just to talk shit with another, fellow female, someone my around my age whom I could really relate to. I would always hold Hank as my number one bestie, but with Anika, it was just so…natural.

Soon enough, we found ourselves at the front of her door. A homemade wreath had been placed outside on a nail, made from a collection of colored paper, pom poms, and pipe cleaners. Surrounding it were pictures scribbled in an assortment of makers and crayons, some of which had greetings written in first-grade chicken scratch.

"I wanted to put her work on the fridge," Anika began. "But Bernie insists that the whole floor should see them."

"Someone's a little artist in the making." I said.

Anika smiled, shifting Bernadette in her arms. "Well...thanks for walking with me. Even if you think turquoise should be with the greens, I think we can still salvage this relationship."

She hadn't said, 'friendship'. Maybe there was hope after all. "Y-yeah! Um, so I guess I'll see you when I see you?"

Anika had already unlocked the door and was pushing it open. But she stopped, giving me a three-second, face-to-face, before nodding. "Yeah. I'd like that. I'm sure Bernadette would like to see you—and Miss Pearlglade—again sometime."

My face got hot as I grinned awkwardly. "Yeah, well...maybe Miss Pearlglade will have a better last name when we meet."

To my surprise, Anika shook her head. "Sometimes your best ideas are the ones we come up with on the spot."

"So, my idea to devour the entire pizza before my Dad could was my *best* idea, then?" I asked.

Anika just coyly grinned. "Goodnight, Rashmi."

"Night, Anika." I gave a little wave to Bernadette, "Night, Bernie."

She gave me another grunt, hand turning slightly to wave as the door gently clicked shut.

Chapter Five

The night would've been absolutely perfect, had I remembered to bring home chicken treats. I completely expected to find a bit of a mess when I came home—it wouldn't be the first time I was greeted to the sight of semi-torn curtains or a small table knocked over—but if I came home empty-handed, Ralsy acted especially cold toward me. Him and Ferguson came bounding out of my room at first, the little kitten skittering around my feet while the big Maine Coon sat down, waiting patiently for his payment.

I knelt, scooping Ferguson up into my arms. "I'm sorry, bud. I totally forgot to pick up some treats on the way home."

Ralsy gave me a puffy hiss, tail shooting straight up as he turned to walk away from me.

"Aw, don't be like that!" I called after him. "It was a bit of a hectic day, all right?"

Briefly, his head turned to me, the expression on his face something like, 'and you think I had it easy?'."

"Fine. Be a butt." I carried Ferguson to the kitchen with me (literally two steps away from the door), pushing him up onto my shoulders while I opened the upper cabinet. Originally, the cat food had been stored on a lower shelf, but kittens had this fascinating power to tear bags open and devour half the food inside (all after dragging it around the house, mind you). Ferguson started losing his mind, pacing back and forth between my shoulders as I pulled out his bright, blue bag.

"Ow, ow, ouch, claws," I winced, quickly putting the bag on the counter as I pulled the Siamese off me. "Dude, come on. I'm not your cat climber; could you not?"

He just wiggled in my arms, trying his best to get to the food.

"Here; you wanna watch me do it?" I glanced around, spotting one of my many abandoned hoodies draped along the back of a chair. One hand stretched across the kitchen to grab it while the other held Ferguson; it was quite a maneuver to try and both put it on and not lose the kitten inside. Finally, my grey hoodie was on, meaning Ferg had the perfect pocket to sit in and watch me. He dropped in like a rock, ears poking out as he thoroughly explored his new setting.

"Mrr-row." Ralsy was suddenly up on the countertop, tail sweeping junk mail off as he eyed me curiously.

"Oh, now you wanna talk to me?" I put my hands on my hips, facing him with my eyes rolling. "Sometimes, I wonder if you just see me as a food machine, Ralsy."

"Mrr-row."

I sighed, pulling and rummaging around shelves for my measuring cups. "Yeah, well, I'm so sorry you had to babysit. I did my own share of kid watching, so you've got nothing to complain about." I didn't really either; Bernadette was an absolute delight to be around. "You'd like her, though. She seems like the type who would lug you around by the pits of your arms."

Ralsy made a noise that was between a mewl and a chitter. It sounded almost questioning, like, 'you'd never let some grubby-handed girl do that to me'.

"Oh, and she'd love you, Ferg." I glanced down at the Siamese, who was fully focused on attacking a lint ball in my pocket. "To be fair, though, I don't know anyone who wouldn't find you cute."

"Mew!" Ferguson glanced up at me, wide eyes shining as a loose strand of string hung around his ears.

"It'd be nice company, too." I finally found my ¼ cup and pulled out Ferguson's special kitten bowl—blue and covered in black fishbone print—before scooping one serving size out. "You two are great, but you're still just boys. And cats," I added, setting the bowl down on the kitchen tile. Ferguson wiggled himself free of my pocket and practically dove head-first into the bowl, spilling half the food as he chomped noisily away.

"Your welcome." I turned to Ralsy next, scooping the big ol' fart into my arms before setting him on the kitchen counter. "Now for you. I'll just keep you up here so Ferg doesn't get to your food. Really don't feel like cleaning up puke again."

I could've sworn Ralsy rolled his eyes. Truly, this cat got me.

Before I could reach for his bowl, someone knocked on my door. It wasn't a two-or-three knock before waiting; this was in rapid-fire succession, like someone banging on the only working bathroom after drinking a gallon of tea. I glanced at Ralsy, only for him to stare back at me. "Look, I don't have friends," I joked while going for the door. "So, if you tried planning a party while I was gone, there's gonna be some words, young man." Ralsy just glared at me, upset I'd interrupted his food prep. Waving him off, I took a brief glance through my peek hole, wondering if I'd forgotten about maintenance coming by. Then, I did a double take.

That was Bernadette, for sure—unless Oak Flats was suddenly hiring minors—standing outside my door with a plastic container in her hands. She was bouncing on her heels, barely able to contain her excitement and hold onto the packed-up food. I quickly opened the door, not seeing hide nor hair of Anika anywhere. "Bernie?"

"Hi, Rashmi!" Bernadette held out the container to me, beaming. "You wanna have a picnic dinner?"

I wasn't sure how to answer that. "Uh...Bernadette, where's your Mom?"

The little girl pointed down the hallway where, to my relief, Anika was just rounding the corner where the elevators let off. "She said I could go ahead and knock, but you came real fast!"

"Well," The word barely left my lips as something small and fluffy darted out between my feet. "Shi—Ferguson!" The Siamese was making an absolute break for it, sprinting down the hallway in that awkward limber all kittens had.

"Uh-oh!" Bernadette dropped the container and rain after him, an explosion of gooey mac-n-cheese erupting all over the place. "I got 'em, I got 'em!"

"Bernadette--!" Anika quickly dropped to one knee and snagged Ferguson by the scruff of his collar. He let out a disappointed yowl, claws scratching in the air as Anika held him out. "Oh, gosh, Rashmi, I'm so sorry."

Wiping away bits of cheese, I jogged down the hallway after them, scooping Ferguson into my arms as he let out a spitting his. "No, that's okay! Good catch, by the way."

Bernadette came running beside us. "Aww! Rashmi, your kitty is so cute! Can I hold her? Can I?"

"Let's let Rashmi carry the kitty back to her room." Anika said. She looked toward my open door, grimacing. "Wow, that's…Bernie, why'd you drop the food like that?"

"I wanted to get the kitty." Bernadette said matter-of-factly.

"Yes, but look at the mess." Anika said.

As guilt crept into Bernadette's face, I hastily added, "Oh, it's not so bad. It'll take a few minutes to clean up, and Ralsy loves cheese more than chicken."

Before anyone could ask, the big Maine Coon was already on the case, having wandered out the door and began licking up the cheddar concoction off the rug.

"You have *two* kitties?!" Bernadette squealed, clearly ready to run head-first into Ralsy. "You gotta be rich!"

A laugh slipped out before I could stop it. "Hah, n-no—I, ah, just like the company."

***

It didn't take long to wipe up the rest of the mess. There were a few dark stains here and there on the outside carpet, but it wasn't anything the cleaners couldn't handle. The walls were wiped clean and quickly, thanks to Bernadette's singing and Ralsy's tongue. Once I dropped off the paper towels, I went about heating up three bowls and took them to the living room. There was one couch, one chair, and a whole ton of cat trees and climbers. Bernadette had long since inhaled her dinner and was delighting herself with my cats. She was bouncing between throwing crinkle balls for Ferguson and petting Ralsy with both hands. She eventually found one of my rod toys, one with a little mouse attached to the string, and both cats were suddenly in full predatory mode.

Anika and I watched for a few seconds, thoroughly entertained. Then, she cleared her throat, setting her half-empty bowl to the side. "So, Bernadette suggested it would be nice of us to gift you with some leftovers. As a way of saying thank-you for today."

"Ah." My attention briefly switched to the fridge, where the remainder of the mac-n-cheese had been stored. "Well, that was awfully nice of you two to do."

"I made it myself! Bernadette said. "Mommy gave me all the stuff to make it with. And she made the noodles," she added as Ferguson dive-bombed the dangling mouse. "But I got to stir them on my step stool."

There was no way in hell I was telling them about my distain for mac-n-cheese now. Back at the hospital, that seemed to be the cook's favorite thing to make (and reheat), so the dish had turned sour for me. Still, my dinner plans consisted of demolishing a whole bag of barbeque chips, so a home-cooked meal was a nice change of pace.

"So," I took another spoonful of mac, semi-playing with it while I looked to Anika. "This 'picnic' thing is typical for you to do?"

Anika laughed. "Bernadette told you that, huh?"

I nodded.

"I'd 'inherited' an old table from my sister, not knowing it was, quite literally, on its last leg." Anika explained. "It broke with an entire Sunday dinner on top of it."

"No." I tried to hold back a grin but failed to do so. "That's *awful.*"

"It was a lot of broken glass and canned vegetables to try and sweep up," Anika laughed. "Douglas took care of the cleaning while I whipped up a few peanut butter sandwiches. Bernadette and I ended up eating them in her room, with one of her blanket's spread out along the floor. We've kinda just…done it ever since." The memory seemed to take her aback; she got this somber look in her eyes, leaning back into the armchair like it would swallow her whole. Bernadette must've sensed the shift, because she was suddenly staring at her mom, rod toy held limp enough in her hand that Ralsy was easily able to bat it away.

"Hey, Bernadette," I stood, an arm around her shoulder as I pointed to the kitchen. "I actually never got to feed Ralsy. Did you wanna help me?"

The light was back in her eyes as Bernadette nodded. I took her to the kitchen, showing her the cup I used to scoop the food and hold the bowl out for her. She carefully held the cup with both hands, slowly inching from the bag to the bowl, all while Ralsy skipped across at the sound of food hitting his bowl.

"Now, Ferguson—that's the kitten—he likes to try and steal Ralsy's food." I glanced around the countertop; right on cue, Ferguson had untangled himself from the rod toy and was bounding across the carpet. "So, I usually put it up here." Before Ferguson could plant his face into the food bowl, I lifted it up on the counter. Ralsy let out a satisfied purr, hopping easily up as he began to pick and chew bits of his food. Ferguson let out a whine and paced back and forth.

"Aww, poor kitty." Bernadette said.

"He's just being a stink." I reassured. "He ate earlier. Here, watch this." I snagged a jingly toy long-since abandoned and held it up to Ferguson. His eyes dilated, ears perking at the sound. I rolled the ball this way and that, laughing as Ferguson's head craned back and forth. "See? He's easily distracted."

"I wanna try!" Bernadette held out her hand expectedly, letting out a squeal when I dropped it onto her palm. She giggled, taking off across the rug as Ferguson bounded after, leaving Ralsy to peacefully eat his meal.

Anika was smiling warmly as I took my seat back. "You sure you don't have your own kid hiding around here somewhere?" she asked.

"Just fur-babies." I said.

"They really are cute." Anika watched her daughter run around with the kitten, smiling wider as Bernadette plops on the ground, dragging the ball around as Ferguson chased after it. "I don't know how I could handle one cat, though."

"Yeah." I roll my eyes and sit back against the chair. "Well, I read somewhere that cats can get lonely at home by themselves, so I ended up adopting Ferguson at a shelter."

"Isn't that dogs?" Anika asked. "Who get lonely by themselves, I mean."

I groaned loudly; she was probably right.

"I think it's sweet." Anika giggled. "I'm sure your other cat...Ralsy, right?"

I nodded, quickly cutting her off. "Before you say what I know you'll say, Ralsy hates him."

"No." Anika laughed.

"No, you're right," I was giggling now, too. "He's completely terrified of him. I've had Ralsy way longer, but he's a total chicken."

As if aware we were talking about him, Ralsy hopped down from the kitchen counter and sauntered over to us, hopping up onto the armchair beside us before curling his tail tight around his body.

"Ooh, is he upset with us?" Anika grinned.

"He's just a big baby." I stood, scooping the Maine Coon up into my arms. He squirmed for a moment but, after scratching in just the right spot on his cheeks, he melted in my arms.

"Oh my gosh, he's huge!" Anika gasped as I sat back down. "I've never seen them get that big."

I grinned, half-holding him out to Anika. "You wanna try holding him?"

"Me?" Anika glanced around the room, like I could've possibly been asking someone else. "Oh, no, I—I mean, I don't want to disturb him. He seems comfortable with you."

"I wanna hold him!" Bernadette scrambled to her feet, the jingling ball dropped on the ground and assaulted by Ferguson.

"Sure. Come sit in the middle, Bernie." I said.

With a squeal, Bernadette hops onto the couch, giving me very little time to scoot and make some room. I gave Ralsy a few more strokes, very gently setting him in her lap. He was purring loudly at this point, perfectly content to sitting on a block of ice at this point. Bernadette's eyes widened, both hands settling on his back. "He's bigger than my whole lap." Bernadette's voice was barely above a whisper.

"Yeah," I said. "Way back when, before people had these kitties as pets, they used to ride on big ol' ships and travel the ocean."

"Really?" Bernadette asked. "But kitties don't like water!"

"Ralsy loves the water!" I swallowed down a laugh as Bernadette gasped. "He sometimes jumps into the bathtub with me, just because he wants to go for a swim.

Anika's brow rose slightly at this, but Bernadette was giggling at this point. "That's silly. You're silly, Ralsy." She added, looking down at my Maine Coon.

He continued purring loudly, paws stretched out as he rolled onto his back.

"Ooh, he's gotta a big tummy." Bernadette gently patted Ralsy's underside, grinning. "You had lots of dinner, huh?"

"Back on ships, he used to chase and eat only rats." I whisper, a maniacal tone in my voice.

"Eww, rat tummy!" Bernadette laughed. "Ralsy don't eat rats."

"Not anymore." I said. "He gets kitty food and chicken treats."

"And cheese." Bernadette added.

Yes. And cheese, though he really shouldn't.

"You know a lot about this breed." Anika points out. Her hand is wavering between petting Ralsy and sticking her hand back by her side.

I chuckled, putting my own hand on Ralsy's abdomen. "Ralsy's been with me for a long time. You know those therapy cats they use in hospitals? The ones to cheer up patients?"

"You sure you're not mixing that up with dogs again?" Anika grinned mischievously.

"No, it's a thing!" I insisted. "There was this big ol' Maine Coon mama who'd come visit me sometimes and she ended up having kittens. I begged my Mom and Dad to let me keep one, and Ralsy hasn't left my side since."

Ralsy just lets out a deep, rumbling purr, delighted to have so many hands pampering and patting him.

"He's real warm," Bernadette yawned loudly, suddenly looking incredibly comfortable underneath her living, breathing blanket.

"Oh, sweetie, are you getting tired?" Anika glanced around for a clock, eventually fishing out her phone with a small gasp. "Gracious—I can't believe it's that late already."

I pull out my own phone at this, confused. 6:25 PM was late?

"It's almost bedtime for you, young lady." Anika started to tuck her arms underneath Bernadette, who tried squirming away.

"Wanna stay here." She grumbled, her own hands wrapping around Ralsy a little tighter.

Anika glanced up at me, a pleading look on her face. Carefully and quickly, I scoop Ralsy off Bernadette and cradle him in my arms; at this point, he was putty. "Wow. I've never seen Ralsy this relaxed. Thanks for helping me get him to bed, Bernadette."

She beamed, flashing me a wimpy thumbs-up as her mom lifted her up onto her hip.

"Well, thank you for having dinner with us." Anika shifted slightly, trying to find just the right amount of weight distribution. I set Ralsy on the couch (he seemed somewhat disappointed) and scooped up Ferguson. Sure, he was playing with his toys now, but the minute we started for the door, that sucker was gonna make a break for it.

"Thanks for bringing dinner up." I said. "Lemme grab the door for you."

"You're not worried about Ralsy?" Anika asked.

I shake my head, chuckling. "Oh, no. That boy's perfectly content staying right where he is."

He let out a lazy yawn in response, stretching out his back and front legs before settling back on the couch.

I reached the door first, unlocking the knob and chain before pulling it open. Even in my hand, Ferguson starts to wiggle, trying to escape.

"He sure is something." Anika shook her head, chuckling.

"He keeps me on my toes." I said. "Like having a toddler."

"I can attest to that." Anika said. "Watching Bernie that age felt like herding cats at times."

We both shared a laugh, trying to be quiet as Bernadette started nodding off against her mom's shoulder.

"Well," Anika stepped halfway out the door, paused, then dipped her head back in. "Thanks again for everything. I...didn't realize how much I needed a night like this."

"My door's always open if you feel like having a 'picnic' again." I was only half-joking; Anika wasn't the only one who really enjoyed this night.

"I might take you up on that offer." Anika grinned, giving me a playful wink before snorting again. "Oh, gosh, that was dumb. I'm sorry."

Now I was cracking up, still trying very hard not to rouse Bernadette. "Go, quick; the night can still be salvaged."

Anika gave an awkward laugh, still snorting behind her hand as she slipped out the door. I gently closed it behind her, my back against the frame. For a moment, I forgot Ferguson was still squirming in my hand. I was still at dinner, reliving the time I'd spent with Anika and Bernadette. How happy Bernie was playing with the cats, how relaxed Anika looked, in comparison to earlier that day. Did this count as a first date? It was kind of weird to have a kid along for the ride, but, I didn't exactly *hate* it.

My phone buzzed in my pocket. I took it out, a warm, fuzzy feeling overtaking me as I did so. It was Hank, spamming my inbox with heart emojis and eggplants and asking if I'd, 'landed the blow'. I shook my head, already typing out my message as I plopped down on the couch, placing Ferguson beside me. The kitten locked eyes with Ralsy, and like that, the two were off, darting around the house and making a general mess of things. I didn't even bat an eye. There was so much erupting in my chest right now, and *someone* was going to experience it with me.

***

After that night, I started seeing the Jenners on a pretty regular basis (and not just because they were literally two floors down). With Bernadette busy with first grade, Anika's week used to be filled with binge-watching rom-coms and sampling the most exotic of bagged chips. It still was, on some days, but with an extra butt on her couch. My butt, much to my delight.

We made sure to mix it up now and again, just so we didn't become lumps on the sofa. Some days, when it was too hot to sit at home, we'd take a walk to Sammy's for a dip (myself insisting that I brought my mermaid gear every time—it's never a bad day to practice). Others, we'd just order pizza and sit outside the complex, completely content to just people watch while stuffing greasy cheese-and-pepperoni into our gobs. Today, however, we ended up walking for almost two hours around the city, with no real destination in mind. Just talking about whatever popped into our heads, each topic spoken with such fluidity, Anika might as well have known me since we were kids. When that subject *did* come about, it was a fascinating treasure trove.

"So, wait," I pulled my lips away from my slurpy straw just long enough to let out a cackle. "You actually shoved your buddy *into* the closet and waited for his parents to come home?"

"Okay, yes," Anika began. "But in my defense, what was *your* first thought when you heard the phrase?"

I shrugged, hand out to take my change as the clerk waved us good-bye. "I can honestly say it wasn't that. His parents took it well, though?"

"I'm pretty sure his Mom was more pissed about him stepping and, subsequently tearing, one of her dress' trains." Anika laughed. "But, yeah. They even helped him ask his guy crush out."

The gas station door chimed cheerfully as we left, making our way back on the sidewalk. It was funny to see our pace was faster than those poor saps stuck in traffic, even when we were waiting for the crosswalk to change.

"His parents sound super cool." I began. "Can't say mine were super receptive at first. They were pretty sure it was just the chemo messing with my head."

Anika's expression shifted from joyful to somber. "That's...I'm sorry, Rashmi."

"Why?" I took another slow sip of my drink, a tingle of cold running down my throat. "*You* didn't make them think that, right?"

Anika's shrug was heavy, her gaze distant. "I dunno. Just feels like someone has to say it."

An uncomfortable silence hung between the two of us as we walked. I should've really gotten a clue years ago and just not brought up any hospital-related stories, but it was hard to leave out a huge chunk of my childhood. I tugged at my straw gently, playing a symphony of squeaks and squonks as it rubbed against the bubble lid of the drink. My eyes shifted toward Anika; she was staring at me, a small smile playing on her face.

"Are you four?" She asked, half-giggling.

"What? This is high-quality stuff, here." I insisted, pushing it closer to her face while moving the straw faster. "I was the first chair staw-ist in my orchestra, you know."

Suddenly, Anika stuck her tongue around the straw, pulling it into her mouth for a quick sip. I froze in place, watching the millisecond exchange while my insides went crazy. Did she just do that? That was like an indirect kiss, right? And she'd initiated it, so, was that the start of requited interest?

My rapid-fire thoughts quickly ended as Anika pushed the drink back against my chest. Her face was scrunched-up, a now-greenish tongue sticking out in mock-disgust. "Oh, God. It's like a soda machine threw up in there."

I was still somewhat stunned. She was so nonchalant about it all; was this really no big deal? "Uh," I pulled the drink away from instinct, a dramatic frown playing along my face. "Well, that's just a matter of opinion."

"But that wasn't even a taste!" Anika laughed. "It's just pure sugar!"

"Which is, arguably, the best taste." I pointed out.

Anika's eyes rolled. Her fingers began to pull at her mass of curls as she began to wind a hair band from her wrist around it. "Yeah, okay. Now I see why you and Bernadette get along." She eventually got her hair to cooperate, pulling it into a high ponytail before letting out a weary sigh. "Some days, I just wanna chop it all off and wear it short."

"I dunno if we could be friends, still, if you did that." I said.

Anika rose a brow at me; briefly, something flashed across her face. Disappointment, maybe? But to which part of my statement?

"Don't get me wrong," I added hastily. "I think you could rock a bob, but you have the two best qualities to hair!"

"You mean a messy, uncontrollable mass that everyone likes to make crack shots at?" Anika's face drew into a puckered scowl, eyes squinting. "You just come off the boat, lassie? Oh, I didn't know leprechauns were so tall!" She groaned, shaking her hair with her hands until it practically stood out in every direction. "I just hope no one at school teases Bernie like that."

"She seems like the kind of kid who'd relish in that sort of attention." I said.

That got Anika to smile. "I won't say you're right, but you're not entirely wrong about that. She gets that from her Dad, I'm certain." Like the wind had been knocked out of her chest, Anika suddenly took a seat at a nearby bench, sat squarely behind a medical pavilion. I followed suit, chucking my now-empty cup into the trash before grabbing a chair beside her.

"You okay?" I asked, clearly knowing the answer. "Maybe we should've grabbed a water bottle for you back at the gas station."

"No, it's not," she shook her head slowly. "I'm not dehydrated." Her fists curled along the table, usually red knuckles going white.

I sat there for a beat, debating if I should bring it up or wait for her to do it. It was weird to think of someone else having a chunk of their life that was awkward to talk about. Throughout the week we'd been hanging out, Anika hadn't really brought up her ex-husband. Douglas, if I remembered the name right. Anytime Bernadette happened to bring him up, Anika would just get so rigid--not outright angry, for Bernadette's sake--but it was like the very name slammed a heavy weight onto her chest.

"Were you the kind of girl," Anika began. "Who'd dream about what your wedding might look like when you became an adult?"

It was a left-field question, but, sure. I was game. "I honestly didn't know if I'd make it that far," I said. "But I watched my fair share of, 'Wedding Dress Dreams' on TV."

Anika giggled, but it wasn't as heartwarming as it usually was. There was some bitterness behind it. "My Mom was a wedding planner for the longest of times. Whenever she couldn't get a babysitter for me—and that was pretty frequently—she'd take me to her office while she talked to clients, or bakeries to sample cakes, or the florist to help pick out flowers. Thinking back," Anika added. "I'm pretty sure I was used as leverage sometimes. A cute little face for the bride and groom to fawn over."

"What a sneaky woman, your mom was." I grinned.

Anika nodded, keeping hold of her own, small smile. "I was a flower girl a few times, actually. For total strangers; can you imagine? I had no idea, of course, I just liked wearing the dress." A dreamy, far-off look crossed Anika's face. "There was just something so...otherworldly about it. I was a part of something, but still just watching it. I hadn't been part of the behind-the-scene stress; I just got to see the end results."

I tapped my fingers against the table, smiling. "You can't tell me you never saw a bridezilla blow up."

"I mean, sure," Anika laughed. "But Ma was pretty quick to send me away. I thought my own wedding would be just as perfect." Her expression fell; I wanted nothing more than to gather her up in my arms and squeeze that sadness right out of her. "Ma didn't quite make it to Douglas' and mine's wedding. Maybe that's why it didn't work out."

That hit me hard in the chest. My own mother didn't even think I'd get to my wedding, so the idea that Anika's situation was reversed shook me. I couldn't even imagine living life without Mami; not yet, anyway. I quickly wiped my face, not even realizing I'd started tearing up.

"Oh, I didn't mean," Anika hastily dug around in her purse, producing a pack of tissues as she handed it to me. "I'm sorry, Rashmi. I shouldn't have brought it up."

I gave her a reassuring smile, accepting the tissues while smearing one or two across my face. "No, it's—my mother says sharing stuff like that strengthens bonds between people. Honestly, I'm honored you trusted me with that."

Anika's own smile returned. "I don't think I've ever heard you talk like that."

"Stick with me for two weeks, and you'll see me bust out some major Shakespeare." I said.

There was the laugh I loved to hear. Anika took her own handful of tissues, suddenly in tears herself. "Oh, my G-God, look at us. Both sobbing like a pair of girls who just broke up with their first partners."

"Not specifically 'boyfriends'?" I asked.

Anika shook her head. "Well, no. You already said you weren't interested in that side of the spectrum, and I swing both ways."

My heart nearly skipped a beat.

"Uh…you okay?" Anika asked. "Your face got really flushed all of a sudden; maybe we should've gotten *you* some water at the gas station.

I waved a hand as nonchalantly as I could. "Ah, yeah! Maybe we should b-both get some water." I waited for Anika to stand first, her glancing around as she began the search for life-bringing H2O. It was fine by me; I was still reeling over this new, tantalizing bit of information.

Chapter Six

"Oh my God, Rashmi! How did you not ask her out there and then?!"

I winced, snatching my phone from my cart as Hank shrieked to the high heavens. In retrospect, putting him on speaker wasn't the best idea, especially as the grocery store was fairly packed. I got double the glares from an elderly couple as I quickly switched the speaker off. "You know she's *still* going through a divorce, right?"

"That excuse is getting pretty old."

"It's not—you should see how much it gets to her!" I sputtered out the words, nearly dropping the box of spaghetti in my hand. "I don't even want to *think* about how much stress being in a relationship would add."

"To which person, exactly?"

Even over the phone, I knew Hank could feel the deadpan energy radiating off me.

"Look, all I'm saying is you could be totally off the mark here."

"Oh, I *want* to hear this one." I tossed the box into my cart, pushing my cart farther down the pasta aisle while scanning prices for marinara sauce. "Please, enlighten me how Anika is desperately waiting for me to ask her out. Because from what I've seen so far, her and relationships tend to mix like a match and gasoline." I opted with a large jar of sauce with meat flavoring, placing it next to the pasta before continuing down the row.

Hank audibly sighed on his end of the phone. *"Divorce isn't the end of the world, you know."*

"It is when said marriage wasn't even graced by your mom's presence."

Hank was silent for a good ten seconds. *"Oh, fuck."*

"And not even because she didn't *want* to go." I pulled a bag of croutons from the shelf, only to quickly put them back when I caught the words, 'Caesar flavored' written across the top. "Anika thinks the marriage fell apart because mom didn't live long enough to help. Did you know she was a wedding planner?"

"Oh, fuck."

"Exactly," I said. "So, what makes you think she'd even want to think about dating--?"

"No, Rashmi," My phone suddenly started blowing up with text messages as Hank managed to stammer out. *"Anika's last name is Jenner, right?"*

"Yeah, but what's that got to do with—"

"Just look what I sent."

I pulled my phone back, flipping through at least a year's worth of texts from him. "Man, I really should clean this thing out," I sighed, thumb growing numb while I skimmed through. A few selfies, some cute pictures of cats, and--bingo.

I nearly dropped the phone there and there.

Hank had sent me a woman's profile for a popular bridal magazine. She was of similar build to Anika, hair more of a muted russet than the firetruck red I'd grown so fond of. Her hair was cropped short, a pair of thin-rimmed glasses set down her nose as she held a clipboard close to her chest. The title read,

'Wedding Must-Haves', and she was square in the center of it. "Oh my God, is that,"

"Analise-Rose." Hank sounded just as stunned as I did. *"Full name; Analise Rose Jenner."*

"That's her mother?!" I covered my mouth, quickly pushing down the canned goods aisle as a few more seething stares came my way. "Oh my God, Hank, oh my *God."*

"If there was a Nobel Prize for wedding design, I'm pretty sure she would've won it. Twice." Hank said.

"She's a *fucking* all-star!" I could barely contain my shrieks at this point. Parking my cart next to the peaches, I cupped my mouth over the phone, as if afraid anyone would hear some deep secret I was about to share. "Hank, you can't be serious. It's has to be just a coincidence."

Hank was silent. Then, *"They're literal carbon copies, Rashmi."*

I let out a heavy sigh, slumped up against the shelves with the phone cradled between my cheek. "What the hell is Anika doing, living in a rathole apartment like that? She could literally claim her job was binge watching at home and *still* make more than a CEO exec."

"Maybe she doesn't want Bernadette growing up to be a spoiled brat?" Hank suggested.

"That only makes her better, Hank." I groaned, dragging slowly down my face. "I can't stack up to that. No way. Thank *God* I didn't ask her out."

"Okay, but," Hank began. *"Maybe she likes how you don't treat her like royalty?0"*

"'Liked'. As in, 'past-tense'." I said. "How the hell can I ignore that, now? I thought dealing with her ex would be awkward, but now I get to add, 'daughter of super rich and famous wedding planner' to that?"

"I'm telling you, Rashmi, Anika really likes you." Hank reassured. *"And I'm not just saying that as your chemo buddy; every time you two come to visit the parlor, it's like the sky parted for God's spotlight on you two. If you had an ounce--an iota--of the confidence you had while being Pearlglade, this wouldn't even be a conversation."*

My heart dropped into my chest at Hank's last sentence. "Oh my God, Ira."

"What?"

"The pictures--I was supposed to pick them up today!" My cart zoomed through the grocery store as I made a mad dash to self-checkout.

"What is it with you being late for this guy?" Hank asked.

"Oh my God, he's gonna be so pissed." I didn't really want to deal with his shitty attitude today, but part of me was certain Ira would take and use the pictures for his own gain. He was weirdly obsessed with them, so I wouldn't put it past him to do some legal mumbo-jumbo to cut me out completely. "Come on, the barcode is right there!"

I could hear Hank snickering on the other end as I desperately tried getting the pasta to scan. *"Just ditch it, Rashmi!"*

"I gotta make spaghetti for Anika and Bernadette tonight!" I snapped back.

"How the hell does that not count as being—"

I hung up as one of the store reps started my way. The last thing I needed was to be banned from the only grocery store for miles.

***

I ended up having to take three buses (one of which decided to just completely pass me over, even though I was standing *right* underneath the sign) to get to Ira's studio office. The man continued to surprise me; I'd fully expected some grungy, studio apartment complex, but instead, I found myself walking around the shopping district before finding an actual building of business. Black brickwork stood as a stark contrast to the white molding, a few flowering plants perfectly cut and framed around the front entrance. I wasn't sure why, but I'd always just associated Ira's business with his name instead of, well, the actual name of business. But now, with big swooping cursive spelling out the name, 'Photo Semblance', it would forever be associated as such.

At least his business was next to a hipster-looking coffee shop. The universe was somewhat righted by that fact alone.

I pushed my way in, greeted by the sound of tinkling wind chimes propped just above the door. The guy behind the front desk glanced up from his skeevy-looking magazine, quickly stowing it away as I approached. "Hi there! How can I help you today," He paused, giving me a quick look-over while visibly racking his brain. Guess he couldn't tell what one of the hundreds of pronouns we had nowadays to address me by.

"Rashmi Machelle," I said. "I'm supposed to pick up some physical copies of my shoot."

The relief washed over the guy's face. "Oh, okay! When was the session?"

"A week or so ago. At Sammy's Swimtime?" I said.

He ticked away on his computer keys, screen reflecting off his glasses. "Yeah, okay...you came at just the right time. We usually start shutting the printers down around now, but I can get this to you in a jiffy."

Who the hell turns off their work equipment at 4:30pm? "Thanks again."

He nodded, clicking a few more times before his face lit up. "Oh! You're the mermaid girl, aren't you? Ira was raving about these shots when he came in; said it's some of the best he's ever taken."

"Really?" They couldn't be that good, could they?

As if to prove a point, the guy turned his screen toward me. It was a scene I knew all-too well, when I'd first met Bernadette. The picture didn't do the panic I felt at the time justice, but damn, did it ever look majestic. Otherworldly, even. Bernadette's arms were reaching down to me, a curtain of bubbles cascading from her initial leap. My arms were outstretched, just barely around her waist, my tail in a semi-arch to show the act of motion. He'd even captured Bernie's look of pure joy-slash-terror as I approached.

"Wow," Was all I could manage.

"It sure is something." The guy shook his head, turning the screen back to his side. "I dunno how he does it sometimes. Like, between you and me," he leaned in close, voice barely above a whisper. "I think the guy's one beer short of a six-pack, but who cares if he can make work like this?"

I admit, he got a giggle out of me.

"Rashmi, Rashmi..." the guy's fingers drummed along the desk, a scowl settling onto his face. "Wait, there was something else regarding you."

There was?

"Ira specifically mentioned it, but," He sighed, shrugging his shoulders. "I'll have to breach the lion's den to ask. Wait here, okay?"

I nodded, taking a seat while desk guy slipped out and wandered to the back. If I didn't swing for the ladies' team, he'd be a candidate for consideration. Sorta wish I'd grabbed his name; maybe Hank would be interested.

I casually reached for one of the magazines, absentmindedly flipping through as my phone buzzed. Speak of the devil. His text was void of the usual emojis and moving pictures, a sure sign of genuine worry.

Please tell me you made it on time. :0

No worries. Got a solid 7.5 on the case.

Noooo, you cheater! >:(

Don't give up on your 9!

Still holding out for a miracle. That rating's for you, anyway.

I glanced back at my magazine, already predicting an essay's worth of questions from Hank about the guy-in-question. For the second time that day, I nearly dropped my phone. There was an article about the evolution of the photography industry, where it was headed thanks to technology and the 'new generation's creative mark', but that wasn't what caught my attention. There was Analise-Rose again, far older than the picture Hank had originally sent me. Standing next to her, though, was a familiarly scruffy face. He looked a bit younger, more disheveled, but there was the same air of self-importance around. It was Ira

I didn't even get to read Hank's response. As if summoned, a pair of shoes came thundering down the hall as Ira's face popped around the corner. His hair was barely put-together, half pulled into a man bun while a camera swung dangerously around his neck. "You!" He jabbed a finger at me; I genuinely flinched. "Mermaid girl!"

"It's Rashmi," I began correcting him. "And I haven't been a 'girl' for almost a decade, so, could we try for the proper terms, here?"

"I don't have time for your PC bullshit, lady." I'd accept, 'lady', but Jesus, what was up with him? "Come to the back with me."

I gave him an incredulous look. This was 100% the start of a kidnapping movie or some snuff film, or both. "I'm sorry?"

He practically leaped to my side, down on one knee as he took my hand. Okay, *now* it was the start of the worst proposal ever. "I got this brat in the back--won't sit still for anything--but you can do it."

"Do *what?*" I pulled my hand free, two seconds away from introducing him to the toe of my sneakers. "Could you *try* and pull your head out of your ass long enough to make sense?"

Ira straightened up, checking the lens of his camera as he continued to talk. "Look, I'll convince them to let you keep some photos for your blog or whatever."

"It's not a blog," I began.

"I'll pay you, too." Ira added. "A hundred bucks for every hour you put up with the brat."

I blinked, somehow more taken aback than I already was. The guy from behind the counter slid back into view; I shot him a look, trying to gauge how serious Ira was right now.

"It's for one of our top clients." he explained. "They want pictures of their niece, but she won't stop crying."

"What does that have to do with--?"

"She's watched, 'The Fishy Princess' enough times to burn out the DVD."

Oh. That was a level of dedication--obsession?-- even *I* lacked when I was younger. "Okay, but I don't have my stuff with me."

"You can borrow anything you want from wardrobe." Ira, again, grabbed my hands and folded them into his. "Please, lady. I was on my knee and everything."

Yup, and it was still super-creepy. "You gonna be back there with me?" I asked, pulling a hand away to point at behind-the-desk guy.

"Me?" He looked around, searching for anywhere else in the room aside from himself.

"I want a witness if shit gets weird." I pulled completely away from Ira now, marching up to desk guy while extending a hand. "You got a name?"

Still stunned, he managed to shake. "Eric."

Sweet. Now I had a name for Hank. "Great; welcome to the crew, Eric. Just hold Ira together and we'll get along swell."

That little girl was possibly more obsessed with mermaids than I was. The minute I got inside the room dressed as the part, her red, tear-stricken face immediately turned up into an ear-to-ear grin. She couldn't be any older than four, hair pulled back in tight-looking pigtails while sitting on a makeshift beach set up behind a greenscreen. Some of the crew slowly unplugged their ears, an instant look of relief on their faces.

"The girl's name is Emily," Eric whispered to me. "And the aunt is Teresa."

I nodded, catching a glimpse of said aunt off to the side. She had piles of toys and goodies to try and distract little Emily from her tantrum, though judging by what I assumed was the discarded pile, it hadn't gone over well. Her expression turned to confusion upon seeing me, but Ira quickly crossed the room and began whispering in a low tone to her.

"Okay; wheel me over to Emily." I said.

Eric nodded, pulling the makeshift wagon we managed to scrounge up in the back room. I made sure to keep the tail out from underneath the wheels, giving a gentle wave to the toddler. "Hi, Emily! I heard you were having your picture taken today; mind if I join you?"

Little Emily let out a delighted squeal, scrambling to her feet as sand flew out from underneath. "Mermaid, mermaid!"

"That's right," I carefully slid myself off the wagon and onto the sand, encompassing Emily with the length of my body. My arms reached out, helping her sit within the crux of tail so she wouldn't completely wipe out from sheer adrenaline. "Your Aunt Teresa gave me a call and I came as quick as I could." I glanced over at said Aunt; Ira must've explained everything, because she was nodding and giving me a smile that clearly said, 'I-will-pay-you-anything-to-keep-her-happy'. "Do you want to take a picture with me?"

Emily nodded furiously.

"Okay! You sit right there then, and we'll smile a big, mermaid smile!"

Ira took that as his cue. He was everywhere around the room, instructing his crew in a hushed whisper while taking rapid-fire shots from his own camera. After a few seconds, I realized I was in charge (again) of positioning and poses. "Hey, Emily, is that a bucket and shovel over there? Let's build a sandcastle with it."

The crew stepped in to give me whatever I needed—water to get the sand wet, seashells to add to the sandcastle, toy crabs to pretend to be the princess of the beach—and Emily was completely enamored. Her aunt was even more thrilled, her smile persistent up to the last few minutes of the session.

She carefully crept over to Ira as he took the last few shots, whispering something into his ear. He paused and looked her way, posture completely straight and face twisted up in surprise. It wasn't something I was used to seeing.

"Tadaa!" Emily held the shovel up in the air to show off her fully built palace of sand. "Is all done!"

I clapped lightly, grinning from ear to ear. "Oh, Emily! That's such an amazing castle! You're going to have to build all my mermaid friends."

The sheer pride on Emily's face was almost too much for me to take. Luckily, Aunt Teresa came over and took her hand, saying something about being time to change.

"I 'anna stay with mermaid!" Emily stuck her lip out into a pout, eyes wide and already filling with tears.

"Well, why don't you invite the pretty mermaid," Aunt Teresa paused, stifling an embarrassed chuckle. "I'm so sorry, I didn't ask your name."

"Call me Pearlglade," I said.

Aunt Teresa's smile widened. "Well then, why don't you invite Pearlglade to your birthday party, Emmy-dear? I'm sure Mummy would be okay with it."

Emily's eyes went wide as dinner plates. She grabbed my hand with her free one, squeezing it with tiny fingers while bouncing up and down. "Please, please, *please?* Will pretty mermaid Pearlglade come to birfday? I'mma have rainbow cake!"

I laughed heartily, doing my best to arch myself upright so we were face-to-face. "Oh, that's my favorite flavor! I would be happy to come."

"I'll leave my contact info with Ira," Aunt Teresa said. "It's this coming Saturday. Thank you so much again." She then reached into her purse and pulled out an impressively thick wad of bills. "Consider this a tip and advanced payment. I can't thank you enough for stepping in today; my sister really wanted a beach theme for little Emily's album. She's," her nose scrunched up slightly. "Very particular."

"You don't say?" I shot a quick glance at Ira, nodding. "I've...had experience with that."

With one more 'thank-you', Aunt Teresa led little Emily to the changing rooms, leaving me alone with the crew, Eric, and Ira, who I was convinced had gone catatonic at some point. He was just sitting on one of the stools, eyes glazed over while his thumb mechanically flipped through the shots he'd taken.

"Wow," Eric offered me a helping hand to sit up. "I don't think I've ever seen Ira so engrossed before."

"Really?" I began carefully working the *incredibly expensive* tail off my legs while glancing up at Eric. "He was that crazed-looking at the pool, too."

"No kidding?" Eric rubbed the back of his neck, a low whistle slipping out. "You must be something special. I mean, those pictures of you before were really good, don't get me wrong, but *this* Ira hasn't come out since Analise-Rose passed away."

There she was again. "Did he know her personally?" I asked.

Eric nodded. "She founded this company from the ground-up. Gave it to Ira based on his talent alone, and after she died," he sighed, suddenly looking somber. "I dunno. It's been awhile since he was this excited. You must remind him of his time with Analise."

"Hey, Rashmi," Ira was suddenly by our side, eyes still glued to his camera. "You got anything else to do today?"

I almost didn't register that he'd used my name. "Uh, I mean,"

"Cause I've got a couple of other clients coming in today," he continued, totally breezing past my attempt at responding. "Would love to get a picture with you in your get-up. Maybe some other costumes, too, if you're not totally set-in-stone with just being a mermaid."

I kinda was.

"I'll pay you for your time, just like now," Ira added. "And I'll mention you're free for gigs. That's a lot of network-gain for a nobody like you."

"That includes us," Eric quickly cut in, clearly seeing the rage building in my face. "We've got a list of call-in models for shoots; I'm sure Ira would be happy to add you to it."

Ira looked ready to object, but the look from Eric gave him pause. I looked between the two, surprised at the sudden shift in power. Maybe Hank didn't have as much of a chance as I thought.

"Yeah," Ira finally said. "I'd do that. But you gotta help out tonight."

Tonight? Like, well into the night-tonight? I bit my lower lip; this was supposed to be pasta night with the Jenners and I was cooking. It wouldn't be right to just cancel last-minute, especially since I'd already bought all the ingredients.

The cash in my hand suddenly weighed heavily in my palm. I could make that, plus more, if I stayed. And I wasn't stupid; getting on Ira's 'model list' or whatever could be an amazing opportunity. It was one night, right?

"Lemme just make a call," I said. "I gotta let some folks know what's going on."

Ira shrugged. "I don't really care who you talk to, long as your back in five for wardrobe and make-up." With that, he promptly turned away, lost inside that massive, ego-inflated head of his while looking through the photos from the previous shoot.

Chapter Seven

It had been a solid minute since I stepped back out to the lobby. My phone was in hand, thumb hovering over Anika's number while I wrestled with every aspect of my being. Pasta Night was something I'd been looking forward to all week, having been officially established after the mac-n-cheese disaster. It was completely by accident too, an offered made by me in the heat of the moment. As hopeless as I was in the kitchen, any simpleton could boil water and watch noodles cook. It seemed the perfect dinner 'date' option, slowly pushing me closer into Anika's embrace.

But this was something else entirely. Not only was I getting offered a job, it was a job with extra perks attached. The more photos I took, the more people would see me. And that meant more gigs, more exposure, more money; my ultimate dream of being a professional mermaid was blossoming before my eyes, today, right now.

"God, a real Sophie's choice..." With a heavy sigh, I pushed Anika's contact info. I put it up to my ear, reasoning over and over with myself that this was the right call. There would be other Pasta Nights. This was a once-in-a-lifetime opportunity.

The phone rang twice before she picked up. *"Hello, Ms. Jenner speaking?"*

Anika's voice almost broke me. Why was this so hard? "Hey, Anika. It's Rashmi."

"Oh, hey!" Anika immediately perked up, warmth and familiarity flooding her voice. *"You ready for tonight? Bernadette's so excited to play with Ralsy and Ferguson again. She used her allowance to buy them one of those little plush mice."*

A squirm of guilt ran through my stomach. "R-Right. Um, about that,"

Anika must've sensed what was about to come. *"Did something happen? I mean, it's absolutely no pressure at all if you don't want to do it,"*

"N-no no! I was totally ready to cook you a mean spaghetti tonight." God, why was this so *hard?* "I just—when I went to pick up my photos today, I sorta got roped into something."

"Well, that doesn't sound illegal in the slightest." Anika's snicker sent my heart into a flurry; only recently had I gotten to see that slick wit. *"What was it?"*

"It was the craziest thing! There was this kid, and she kept crying—I got to dress up as Pearlglade and got *paid* for it." Was I actually excited to talk about this? It was nice to tell someone. Only now, one it was all said and done, did it really sink in how amazing this opportunity was.

"Whoa, really?" It warmed me up to hear Anika equally excited. *"Rashmi, that's awesome!"*

"The photographer wants me to stay and do a few more sessions," I continued, barely able to speak straight. "I got asked to show up at a party, and—God, it's just so much at once, but I feel awful for picking it over,"

"No, no! Rashmi, this is a great opportunity." There was a hint of disappointment in Anika's voice, but she oozed with overwhelming positivity and support. *"I'd never want to come between someone and their dream."*

That last part stung more than I thought. I know it wasn't intentional, but somehow, my chest still ached. "Y-Yeah."

"You know what? Why don't we bring the dinner to you?" Anika asked. *"Even a famous model has to be given a break; I'm sure Bernadette will be thrilled to have pizza tonight."*

It was almost too perfect to believe. "Oh my gosh, yes! That's a great idea." Anika had to be sent from heaven, she was so reasonable and understanding. Somehow, I'd gotten everything I wanted tonight and more.

"All right! I'll let Bernadette know the change in plans. We'll see you in an hour or so?"

I nodded, then, realized Anika couldn't see that. "Yes, absolutely."

"I'll see you then!" With that, Anika hung up, leaving me in silent, tingling euphoria. I'd expected her to be upset, to call the night off while trying to sound happy for me, like some cheesy romcom. But this was real life, and Anika had more sense than some blonde-haired floozy on TV. No; we wouldn't have Pasta Night but eating pizza with them while boosting my mermaid profile was the next best thing. Possibly even better.

And then the front door swung open, nearly taking out my shins.

"Where's my 7.5?" Hank stumbled in, breathless, looking around the lobby like a cat in heat. "You can't just say that and go totally dark on me, girl!"

Oh, God, I'd totally forgotten. "Sorry about that," I gestured Hank to a chair, still bouncing with adrenaline. "I'll introduce you in a second, but you'll never *believe* what happened to me." I then quickly regaled the story to him, ready for him to share in my enthusiasm. He was a good listener as always, excited for the right parts and groaning at others. But once I got to the part with Anika, his expression shifted.

"Wait," he began. "So, you're not doing Pasta Night?"

"Well, no," I said. "But Anika's fine with it. She's gonna bring Bernadette and pizza over to the studio. It's the best of both worlds!"

"I mean, I guess."

I could feel the frown tugging at my lips. Hank wasn't as thrilled as I hoped he'd be. "What?"

"Nothing." Hank's face said a different story.

"You wanna say something," I said.

He let out a loud sigh, something he'd clearly been holding in for a while now. "Rashmi, the dinner thing was special! Way more intimate than eating around a greasy, cardboard box at some snobby photo-gallery."

"Sure, but she was fine with changing plans," I said.

"Only because she'd look like a total monster for making you choose between her and your career." Hank shook his head, as if that was common knowledge I should've known.

"So, *I* have to choose between the two?" I asked, hoping the irritation was clear in my voice.

"I mean," Hank shrugged, glancing down at the magazines on the table. "You already had plans."

"Yeah, and plans change." My arms crossed over my chest as I huffed. "Seriously, Hank? I thought you'd be happy for me."

"I am!" Hank's attention snapped back to me. "Of course, I am. I just,"

"Just trying to run my life for me?" I stood, a fresh wave of anger coursing through my body as I loomed over Hank. "Like you've been doing ever since we met?"

"Whoa, wait," Hank stood now, visually and vocally taken aback by my sudden shift in mood. "Where's this coming from?"

"*You're* the one who said I should chase my dream!" Even I was surprised by how venomous my tone had gotten, but it was too late. I was already in it, vision flashing red while my voice grew louder. "*You're* the one who said I needed purpose after remission, only to tell me I just *had* to chase after a woman I was perfectly content leaving as an unrequited crush. And now I'm doing my best to make it work, but you're *still* telling me I'm doing it wrong!"

"I never said—!" Hank stumbled over his words, looking equal parts furious and hurt. "I'm trying to be a good friend. You gotta be careful with these things, balancing aspirations and relationships. If one gets thrown out of whack, you're gonna regret it!"

"The only thing I'm regretting right now is talking to you during my first chemo run."

Hank looked visibly sick, like someone had just punched him in the stomach. The words had come out way too fast for me to process, but once they were out there, my tongue went numb. "Wait, Hank."

He stormed past me, throwing the door open without a second's hesitation.

***

Three days.

It had been three days since my fight with Hank. He'd completely ghosted me, refusing to answer my texts or call me back after the hundred or so voicemails I'd left him. It'd gotten to the point where calling him just resulted in a robotic voice telling me his inbox was full.

Telling me to, essentially, fuck off.

Anika had been incredibly supportive through it all, reassuring me that he just needed space, that a real friendship wouldn't break over a little spat. Of course, I'd failed to tell her the *exact* details of the fight, only that we'd had one. I couldn't even remember a time him and I had an argument, if ever. Hank was always the positive presence, someone I turned to after the world was done throwing me around. Always smiling, always ready with a sharp comeback or cheering me on when something good happened in my life.

Just like back in our hospital days.

***

"You look like you've seen a ghost."

I looked up from my balled-up fists at the boy who spoke to me. He looked like one of the bigger kids from the other ward, his face looking like one of the plastic skull decorations from Halloween. He was hooked up to his own seat while his feet slowly, rhythmically, swung and bumped against the front of the chair. He didn't have any hair, just like a lot of kids I'd seen in this place, but it wasn't because I could see what was on top. It was because he had a bunch of colorful scarves wrapped around.

"Wh-why you wearin that?" My voice jumped an octave as something sharp pricked my arm. Hot tears started running down my face, but they quickly stopped as the boy laughed.

"What, these?" He gestured to the scarves with a twirl of his finger. "It just didn't seem fair, is all. All the girls get to wear pretty ones, and I deserve to look pretty, too."

Now that he said it, I had noticed other kids wearing those scarves around their heads. Girls especially. "But, they're girly." His were especially so, a mix of purple and pink with flowers scattered across.

"So?"

My brow scrunched up; this wasn't making sense. "You can't wear it, then!"

"Says who?"

I opened my mouth, but no name came to mind.

"I think you're just jealous." The boy snickered. "You want this one all for yourself."

I shook my head, scowl heavy on my face. "Nu-uh! It looks dumb."

"Does not." The boy said.

"Does too!" I snapped back.

"Does not."

"Does too!"

"All right, Hank," My nurse suddenly stood, shooting the boy a look. "That's enough out of you."

"What? I was doing you a favor." The boy—Hank—pointed to my arm, where an IV had seemingly appeared from nowhere. *"See? She didn't even notice you do that."*

He was right.

"Well, your methods could certainly be less argumentative." The nurse said.

Hank scoffed weakly, leaning back in his chair.

As the nurse started out the door, I found my curiosity peaked. "How'd you do that?"

"Do what?" Hank was still leaning back, but the delight on his face was clear.

"I didn't even feel the needle," I said with a squint. "You got magic powers or something?"

Hank gestured to the scarf with a devilish grin. "Just a magic scarf."

"Nu-uh. You're lying." I said that, but man, was I hooked now. "Where'd you find it?"

"You really wanna know?" Hank's voice dropped to a low whisper. "It's a secret only big kids get to hear."

"I'm a big kid," I insisted. "I'm ten and a half."

Hank let out a whistle. "That does fall under the big-kid clause. Just barely, but I'll make an exception. Don't tell anyone else, though, okay?"

I nodded, partially leaning forward in my seat.

"Okay." Hank settled deep into his seat, sleepy-eyed and shoulders sagging. "This is a legend passed down from kid to kid. It all started in Room 203..."

***

"Hey, Rashmi! Rashmi?"

I blinked, suddenly back in the coffee shop Anika and I stopped at. "Uh, sorry. What were you saying?"

Anika sighed, pushing her cup of fruity-smelling tea to the side. "This Hank stuff really has you in a tizzy, huh?"

I stirred my straw around my iced coffee, unable to stop myself from slumping over the table.

"Oh, Rashmi," Anika took my free hand into hers, smiling sympathetically. "You two will work it out. I just can't see a friendship like yours falling apart this easily. Thick as thieves, you two are!"

She'd reached for my hand. I couldn't stop a nervous giggle from slipping out. "Wh-who says that anymore?" I asked, voice slightly pitched.

"I do," Anika gave my hand a squeeze, only sending the butterflies in my stomach into a fit. "And I mean it. Thing's work out, which isn't something I thought I'd ever say."

It really wasn't. The Anika I knew almost two weeks ago was worried about every little thing, determined to believe that life had it out for her. Now, she seemed so relaxed, exuding a bright, positive aura I found myself severely lacking the past few days.

"I take it the hearings have been going well?" I asked.

Anika leaned back in her chair, taking her cup back in hand as a small grin crossed her face. "The judge isn't exactly thrilled with Douglas' dine-and-dash from the ice cream parlor. My lawyer's pretty confident about our chances of getting sole custody." She took a sip of her tea, voice softer than before.

"Still...I'm not sure if that's the right thing to do. He's still Bernie's father, and she still loves him, and the very *last* thing I want to do is force her to choose. That's something I swore would never happen, given I ever had kids."

An interesting tidbit, but not one worth pushing. "That means you're a good Mom," I offered reassuringly. "Thinking about what Bernadette might want, I mean."

"But Douglas is just so," Anika's hand started to tremble, tea threatening to spill out and over the rim. "I mean, he's infuriating! Whatever part of me fell for him is dead and buried, and to think he could influence Bernadette as she grows up just—just makes me so--!" she let out a pained gasp, tea cup crashing to the ground as her hand involuntarily flinched from hot liquid managing to, at last, escape.

I nearly fell out of my seat, quickly gathering as many napkins as I could. Half-stumbling around the table, I ignored the pieces of porcelain on the ground, rushing to Anika's side to try and clean up the mess.

"I'm okay, I'm okay." Anika nodded her thanks, the spot on her hand quickly flushing red. "Thanks, Rashmi. I guess I'm still not over it all just yet."

An employee had noticed the trouble and quickly gathered a few others around her, saying something about a broom and garbage can. I took that as my cue to just take care of Anika, partially hovering over her chair while the staff went about picking up the mess. "You don't have to be over it," I began. "I mean, I dunno what Douglas did to invoke your wrath, but it doesn't matter. You can still be hurting over it."

Anika nodded. "It's just...scary to think about. Potentially raising Bernadette by myself; I never wanted to make the same mistake as *my* Mom, but here I am." She sniffed, quickly wiping her eyes with the sleeve of her shirt. "Goodness, there I go again."

"That's okay, too." I took her hand this time, giving her my most reassuring grin. "You're not alone, either; I'll be right here if you ever need anything."

Anika's smile set my insides on fire. It was the sort of smile I cherished, wanted to protect with every inch of my life. "I really appreciate that. Honestly, this would all be so much harder without you here." She suddenly looked sheepish, hands fidgeting in her lap. "Actually, since you mentioned it, and it's completely up to you but," Anika paused, then shook her head. "Ah, no. Never mind."

"You better come out and say it," I began, smirking. "I'll flood your inbox otherwise."

She laughed, moving out of her chair so the employees could wipe up the mess underneath. We both gave a quick reassurance to the staff that everything was fine, it was just an accident, and no, Anika didn't need to be taken to the hospital over this. As we left the café, she finally spoke up about her request. "It's just, well, there's another custody hearing coming up soon, and my lawyer suggested to have witnesses talk about what happened that day at the parlor. Plus," she added with a grimace. "I heard Douglas is bringing quite the support, so having someone on my side would be nice."

My first major event with Anika. Granted, it was in the most boring place on earth, but for her, I'd watch paint dry. "Of course I'll be there. Just tell me the day and time."

"You sure?" Anika asked. "I asked Hank previously if he could drive us, just so I know I wouldn't be late."

"I can't promise we'll be best buddies again," I began. "But we can for-sure put our baggage aside for a fellow friend."

Anika looked instantly relieved. "Thank you so much, Rashmi." She glanced down at her wristwatch, nodding to herself. "Well, school's gonna be out, soon, and the party's right after. Ready to go get Bernadette?"

"Yeah," I said. "With two sexy numbers like us working together, we'll get a taxi in seconds."

Anika snorted with laughter. "I don't know about that, but I still like our odds. Let's go."

Chapter Eight

The fact that Bernadette had been invited to the same party I was mermaiding at was an incredible coincidence. In truth, I'd been pretty nervous going to my first gig without a face to recognize in the crowd, but with the Jenners there, my confidence was an all-time high.

Our taxi pulled around the cul-de-sac before coming to a stop at the designated address. It was a typical, cookie-cutter setup, every house painted an offshoot white and roofed with charcoal-grey tiling. This one seemed especially organized, with every flower planted in color order, every bush and plant trimmed to uniformed perfection. "Woof." I slid out of the taxi first, eyeing up the place with a frown. "Aunt Teresa wasn't kidding; her sister *is* a perfectionist."

Bernadette came shooting out of my side while Anika opened the opposing door. She was dressed to the nines in a big, poofy dress, colored like summertime grass with a neat, lime-green bow wrapped around her waist. Her shoes—a nice pair of brown buckle-ups—refused to stay in place as she began circling around the driveway. "Mommy, Mimi, come on!"

I couldn't help but grin; 'Mimi' was the nickname Bernadette had started addressing me by and I was adoring every second of it. It had randomly popped out of her mouth one walk around the park and had stuck since. Though, I wasn't sure if Anika had picked up that my new nickname sounded *a lot* like, 'Mama'. Or, maybe she knew and was totally cool with it.

Which meant my chances getting together with her would only grow stronger.

"Wonder if Teresa's here today?" Anika wondered aloud. "I always got along with her better than her sister."

"So you *do* know the birthday girl's mother?" I asked, snagging my backpack out the back of the taxi.

Anika gave me the universal, 'so-so' sign with her hands. "I can't really see myself as a friend of hers, but I hung out with Teresa a lot in high school. Millicent and I became familiar by proxy."

"Millicent, huh?" Anika must've seen the grin on my face, because I was quickly punched in the shoulder. "What? She has the perfect old-lady name once she reaches that age."

"Everyone calls her Millie," Anika began. "And if you wanna get paid for this, I suggest you call her that, too."

After we split the cab fare, the Jenners and I walked around the width of the property, hearing party noises located off in the back yard. We arrived with a quick walk and the unlocking of a white-picket fence. Balloons and streamers were sprawled out across the lawn, everything themed around one thing and one thing only; mermaids. There were seashell tablecloths, a bounce-house whose inflatable pillars were fishy tails sticking upward, and a pinata dangling above the only tree in the yard that was the Fishy Princess herself. Bernadette's eyes went wide, trying her best to take in the scene. Truthfully, I was a bit stunned as well. These folks really *were* rich; all I got for my birthdays were a cupcake and a pair of socks.

"Anika!" Aunt Teresa waved us over, situated at the gift table with a glass of what I could only guess was the 'special' punch.

"Hey, Teresa!" Anika waved back, eagerly scooting around hordes of small children to embrace her old buddy in a hug. A twang of jealousy ran through me at their embrace. I took Bernadette's hand and made our way over, making doubly sure Auntie dear saw us.

"I'm so glad you made it," Aunt Teresa arched over, hands on her knees as she beamed at Bernadette. "Berna-dettie! Well, don't you just look so grown up in that dress."

Bernadette held the hem of her dress in hand, grinning madly. "Mommy got it special for today. She's gonna smack my butt if I get it messy."

Anika's face lit up as her arms pulled Bernadette to her side. "Haah, kids! They say the darndest things."

Teresa's brow rose, but she let out a hearty laugh. "Well, that's why God invented stain remover, right?"

"Yeah!" Bernadette's head tipped up to her Mom as she repeated matter-of-factly. "That's why God made stain 'mover."

"You aren't helping," Anika said, her lip stuck out in mock-pout.

God, but wasn't this awkward. Nothing worse than watching two close friends catch up. Their chemistry felt so natural, like they'd picked up right where they last left off. But I wasn't *actually* worried, was I?

Was I?

"Oh, right!" Aunt Teresa turned her attention toward me, as if sensing my awkward presence.

"You're here! Don't tell me," she squinted, finger tapping on her chin. "Rashmi, right?"

I nodded, "But my fishy friends call me Pearlglade."

"Mimi turns into a mermaid when she gets wet!" Bernadette cried excitedly, beginning to bounce under her mother's embrace. "It's so, so cool!"

Aunt Teresa nodded, laughing. "So I've heard! Actually, Berna-dettie, that's why I invited Miss Rashmi today."

A squeal slipped out of Bernadette as she darted toward me, arms wrapping around my waist. "You're gonna be a mermaid today, Mimi?"

"Uh-huh." I said. "Hope you didn't wanna go on the bounce house with me."

"Naw; only kids get on that, anyway." With that said, Bernadette immediately turned back to her mom, eyes wide and pleading. "Mommy! Can I go on the bouncy house?"

A brief look of worry crossed Anika's face, but Aunt Teresa waved her hand. "Nika, there's like, twenty other adults here. She'll be fine; I bet Miss Rashmi'll need help getting back out here, once she's, ah, 'transformed'."

That seemed to do the trick. "Well, all right. You okay with me tagging along, Rashmi?"

"Are you kidding?" I took her hand, already leading her back to the house. "You finally get to see the magic behind the mystery! I've always wanted to show someone how I got ready."

With a quick wave to Bernadette (who was already kicking her shoes off in preparation for the bounce house), Anika and I passed through the sliding, double doors. I had expected the interior to be classy and covered in white, expensive objects, but Millicent had at least some sense when it came to raising a toddler. Every corner had been softened, all technology put up in out-of-reach places, and every color chosen for ease of cleaning if—*when*—a mess occurred. All in all, it was a pretty nice-looking place, somewhere I could see myself living one day.

"You'd think she wasn't ridiculously rich from the setting." Anika whispered.

I bit back a snort. "That's rude."

"You were thinking it, too." Anika giggled. "And that's a compliment! I think it looks nice. I could see myself living in a place like this."

I gave Anika a stunned look. Was she a mind-reader, now? She just gave me a bemused smile and set off in search of a bathroom. I followed behind, not that I had a choice since we were still holding hands, still taking in the sights.

Until my sight was taken up by a pair of breasts.

Somehow, I'd managed to walk right past Anika and into the chest of another woman. She let out a panicked shriek, pushing me away as I staggered back and nearly lost my footing. Luckily for me, Anika was *still* holding my hand, meaning I managed to stay upright. "O-Oh my God," I managed to stammer something out, hand covering my face. "I'm so sorry! I completely didn't see you there."

The woman just stood there, frozen, as if trying to process what just happened. After a moment, she went about straightening herself out, pulling what I swore was a handkerchief out of nowhere and rubbing it across her semi-exposed chest (not that there was anything to clean; I hadn't put on any make-up yet). "It—it's fine." Her voice was barely above a whisper, as if traumatized by mere contact with me."

"Heeey, Millie." Anika waved awkwardly, semi-pulling me behind her as she greeted the somewhat manic woman. "Great party. Can't believe little Emily's already four."

Millicent just nodded, still rubbing her skin until it began turning red.

"Uh," Anika glanced back at me, grimacing. "Did I introduce you to Rashmi? She's gonna be dressing up as the mermaid."

Millicent looked confused, but only for a moment. "Oh, right. My sister's childish idea."

I couldn't help but frown at this. With the rush of success recently, I'd sorta forgotten that some folks found my job to be, well, childish.

"Still, it's better than hiring a clown." Millicent continued, her words a dagger wedged between my ribcage. "You know she's paying you, right? I don't have anything to do with this, this provocative exposure."

"I brought a number of suits," I started to say, eyeing her own breasts ready to pop out of her number of a dress. "So, I'm not 'exposing' myself to anyone."

"Whatever." Millicent waved a hand and started past us, careful not to touch any part of me (and just me). She then paused, eyes fixated on the top of my head. "You're not sick, are you?"

"Personal choice." I managed to hiss out.

"Good."

With that, Millicent went toward the double doors, sliding them apart with the handkerchief and passing through. I looked at Anika; she looked positively horrified. "Ooh, goodness, Rashmi."

I held up a hand. "It's fine. You gotta be used to folks like that with how I look."

"Maybe, but still." Anika scowled, arms crossing over her less-than-forward chest. "I don't quite remember her being so...*prudish*. A bit OCD, certainly, but that whole scene just now was totally uncalled for."

I chuckled weakly, "Seriously, don't get too twisted up. Hank and I actually make a game out of how many folks..." My sentenced died halfway out of my throat.

Anika must've noticed my shift in mood, because she quickly brightened up. "Hey, didn't you say you brought a whole bunch of suits?"

I nodded, not entirely sure where the conversation was headed.

Anika's face suddenly flushed red. "Well, do you think any of them would fit me?"

Wait, had I heard that right? "You wanna be a mermaid with me?"

"If one fits!" Anika's voice came out as a squeak as she nervously giggled between every other word. "I dunno, I just—I've been opening myself to trying new things lately. Picking a different dish off the Chinese takeout menu, walking a different route to Bernadette's school," she caught a curl of hair between her fingers and started twirling it. "If I'm being honest, I thought you were sort of, well, immature, when I first met you."

Ouch.

"But seeing those pictures of yours, and, well," Anika laughed. "I feel like every little girl wants to be a mermaid when she's younger. I'd long-since given up such fantasies, but after I met you, I dunno. It feels like anything's possible. I want to experience this thing that makes you so happy."

This was unreal. I didn't even really know if my suits would fit her—we didn't exactly have similar body types—but just hearing Anika say those words filled me with a flooding warmth. "Th-that's," Holy crap, was I tearing up? I quickly wiped my face, grinning. "I think I got something that'll fit you perfectly. How's Bernie gonna react, though?"

"What do you mean?" Anika asked.

"You know," I began. "When she learns her Ma was keeping such a big secret from her all these years?"

After a second or two, Anika broke out into a fit of giggles. "Are you kidding me? She'll be asking me for weeks if she's a mermaid, too. I dunno if I'll be able to get her out of the water if I do this."

I offered Anika my hand. She took it wholeheartedly.

"Is that a bad thing?" I asked.

That smile of hers could melt a million polar ice caps. "No, I don't think it is."

***

It usually took me less than five minutes to bring out Pearlglade, but with Anika, extra steps had to be taken. Thankfully, I didn't have to try and show her how to put on a mermaid slip *and* monofin, though the slip persisted in giving the poor woman troubles. At first, I was afraid her bustier build would tear the fabric at the seam, but I'd spared no expenses on getting the best-made mermaid gear out there (or, at the very least, ones that weren't obviously made in some sweatshop). In the end, Anika managed to slide herself into one of my teal-colored numbers, the fin an ombre of darker blues, while the top was a one-piece with a fish scale pattern. I had my now-trademark pink fin, though opted for a one-piece as well in lieu of my run-in with Millicent. All that was left, now, was make-up and accessories.

"Feel free to put whatever in your hair," I was fully focused in the bathroom mirror, making sure my wig wouldn't slip off at the slightest jostle. "With your hair color, braiding some fake seaweed would make everything pop."

"Don't say, 'pop'," Anika moaned, half-slumped against the back of the tub. "I feel like a canned anchovy in this. It's gotta be too small."

"Actually, it should fit a bit snuggly," I said reassuringly. "Theoretically, you'd be swimming in this, too, so it has to act like a suit would."

"Suits are supposed to be this well-fitting?" Anika asked.

I wasn't sure how to answer that. "Here; lemme help you with your make-up." I carefully maneuvered myself to the ground, pulling my backpack to my side while I fished around for my make-up purse. "I'm thinking green eyeshadow, a little bit of sparkles on the cheeks—my stuff's waterproof, but nobody wants it caked on when it's hot out. Plus," I added, finally finding what I needed. "We wouldn't want to upset Millicent's *gentle* disposition."

"Don't tease her," Anika giggled. "It's her party, after all."

"Ah, you're right. This *is* a party for a small child." While Anika broke out into a fit of snickers, I managed to pull out everything I needed. Mascara, rouge, the previously-mentioned eyeshadow— everything was set to turn Anika into a fellow merfolk.

"Oh my goodness," Anika sighed, her giggles contained as she stared nostalgically at the make-up. "It's been years since someone else did my make-up for me."

"No one did it for your wedding day?" I asked, twisting the mascara from its container.

Anika shook her head. "I wanted it to be my Mom, but that wasn't going to be possible."

I was still for a moment, really taking in Anika's mood. This was really special to her, something that probably brought a mixture of sadness and joy to the forefront of her mind. I gave my best smile to her, determined to make this experience a good one. "What would she say if she saw you now?"

"There'd be some questions," Anika chuckled. "But, ultimately, I think she'd just be happy to see *me* happy again."

That was enough for me. "Well, let's get you ready for your first debut, *Sea Lily.*"

Anika laughed, "Is that my own mermaid name?"

"You like it?" I asked. "Just came up with it now."

She smiled from ear-to-ear. "It's perfect. A nice-sounding friend for Pearlglade."

***

Thank God there were adults at this party who could lift more than ten pounds. It only occurred to me *after* we'd gotten dolled up that it was going to be *rough* going back outside. Lucky for me, Anika had Aunt Teresa on speed dial (and her pants were still in the bathroom with us). In a few minutes, we had two, strapping lads carry us bridal style back outside. I took the time to run through a few points with Anika, given this would be her very first time.

"Feel free to let kids touch your fin and stuff," I began. "It's all washable, so we don't fear their grimy fingers. Just don't let them pick or pull at it."

Anika nodded, absorbing every word I spoke.

"Try to stay in character as much as possible," I added. "We don't wanna crush dreams by revealing we're just grown women in suits."

That got a laugh out of her. "Okay, but, what's my story?"

"Your what?"

"You know, my motivation!" Anika's expression shifted, as if she was suddenly deep in thought. "Why did I make my way to the surface? What are my goals, my aspirations? Do I like minty toothpaste, or bubblegum?"

I gave her an incredulous look.

"You said to 'get in character'," she protested. "This is how we did it in theater."

"Well, dial it down to like, a two." I said. "Just, act fantastical, I guess. I dunno; I just sorta was me, but more energetic. Child-friendly."

107

"If that's even possible." Anika said while sticking her tongue out.

I directed us to one of the picnic benches, a swarm of children already following after us. The ages ranged from four to six, but every single one of them looked just as delighted to see us. Once Anika and I settled into our spots, the job official began.

"All right, everyone," Aunt Teresa stepped forward, acting as a sort of barrier between us and them. This may have been Millicent's party, but it was clear who was actually in charge. "If you would take a seat, I'd like to introduce our new friends!" She quickly shot a curious look at Anika, who simply smiled and shrugged back. A mass exodus of parents came to us, gathering their kids up into their arms or pulling them into their lap as they sat down on the grass. I gave a little wave to the growing crowd, Anika following suit, albeit a bit more hesitantly.

Once it seemed like every interested kid was paired with a grown, Aunt Teresa began her spiel. "I'd like to introduce some very special friends from the sea. They came all the way to play and wish Emily a happy birthday. Let's say hi!"

A chorus of 'hi's and 'hello's came from the crowd, partially translated as excited screams from all the little girls.

"Well, what a warm greeting from you all," I began. "Thank you so much for having us. My name is Pearlglade, and this is Sea Lily."

Anika gave another, more confident wave. "Rash—ah, *Pearlglade* and I are so happy to be here. I'm sure we're all going to become great friends."

I gave her an approving nod; not bad for her first time in her scaled persona. But the real fun had only just begun. After Aunt Teresa quickly went over a few interaction rules for us (mainly directed to parents and basically summarizing as, 'don't let your kids pinch or poke the mermaids'), a winding que set itself up, stretching all the way from our bench to the bounce house. The main idea was to pose and smile while moms and dad took pictures, but of course, *talking* to the kiddos was another aspect of the task.

"Can you swim real, real fast?" One pigtailed little girl asked.

"As fast as any dolphin," I responded. "I've won quite a few races against them, but we're still the best of friends."

"Do you talk to fishies?" A blonde-haired girl inquired.

I nodded, grinning. "I do! I like talking to my two catfish. They get into all sorts of trouble when I'm away."

Anika was quick to get into the spirit of her role, though part of me suspected that was due in part to her aforementioned, 'theatrical' experience. She was happy to let parents set their toddlers on their lap, discussing and laughing over the little terrors they were on a daily basis while taking quick snapshots with their phones. It was a more social side to Anika I hadn't been privy to before, like she'd finally found a group of people who understood her and could connect with her tales of motherhood.

Finally, word had spread enough to pull little Bernadette back our way. She'd all but abandoned her shoes back at the bounce house, having been thrown in a bit of a tizzy to have learned not one, but *two* mermaids, had arrived at the party. Only now was Bernadette realizing the other was Anika.

"Y-You're a," She'd been tripping over the same sentence for the past minute or so, way too elated to even speak straight.

"Rashmi showed me how she turned into a mermaid," Anika began. "So I thought I'd try it for myself."

Bernadette's head swiveled to me, next. "You can turn *other* people into mermaids!?"

I shrugged, smiling. "It's kinda a really big secret. But now that you two are my friends, I can trust you with it." One of the mom's gently tapped me on the shoulder to get my attention, her two-year-old in arm. I happily obliged, taking the tiny tot into my lap as mom got ready to take a picture.

"You gotta do it to me!" Bernadette whined, bouncing up and down on Anika's lap. "I wanna be a mermaid, too!"

Anika briefly looked panicked, but I had already prepared for this exact, inevitable request. "You have to learn to swim with your legs, first, before I can give you a fin."

Bernadette's excitement immediately flipped into a sulk. "That's not fair. I'm still learning."

"But you're getting better and better every day," Anika pointed out. "Soon, you'll be ready."

"Can Mimi teach me, too?" Bernadette asked. "I can learn twice as fast if you *and* her did it!"

Her math didn't quite add up to me, but I couldn't say no to her enthusiasm. "I'll mark it on my calendar, Bernie."

Though Bernadette was absolutely thrilled with the response, Anika seemed less-than-certain. I didn't know what it was, but something in me said she didn't quite believe me. Was it because I had said no the last time? But that was then, before we'd all become close. I wouldn't deny this for Bernadette...yet, why was Anika making that face?

Suddenly, Millicent breached from the crowd like the horrifying whale she was. Emily was squirming in her arms, impatiently reaching toward Anika and I.

"Mermaid, mermaid!" She said.

I gave her a little wave, "Hi again, Emily! Thank you for inviting me to your party."

Little Emily was trying so hard to get out of her mother's arms, but Millicent kept a firm grip around the toddler. She then turned completely to Anika, ignoring me entirely. "It's Emily's turn to sit. Not that I need any more pictures of fish people," she added bitterly. "But I suppose my sister would be cross if I didn't play along."

Anika looked confused. "Um, sorry, but I'm talking with my daughter. You remember Bernadette, right?" Her hand rested on little Bernie's head as a flash of something primitive passed behind her eyes.

"I don't care," Millicent said. "It's Emily's turn to sit on your lap."

Anika gestured to me, still being thoroughly ignored. "Rashmi is perfectly able to take photos with Emily."

"But I want *you* to take her."

God the tension was palpable between the two. "I know I'm a stranger," I began. "But I've held hundreds of young children before. I promise little Emily's perfectly safe."

Now I had Millicent's attention, but some part of me really didn't want it. "Don't say her name," she hissed between her teeth.

"*She's* the one you're paying, Millie." Anika's jaw was set, her hands set firmly on Bernadette's shoulders. "Let her do the job you hired her for."

"*I* didn't hire her!" Millicent was practically shrieking at this point. "I would've never hired someone like her in the first place!"

At this point, every head was turning our way, including a very embarrassed Aunt Teresa. She quickly stepped up, doing her best to ease Emily out of her mother's hands, who had started bawling at this point. "Millie, dear."

"Don't touch her!" Millicent pushed away from her sister, only succeeding in completely wiping out beside me. Emily, thankfully, fell on top of her chest, but had broken out into wailing sobs after falling over. With little arms and legs flailing, she managed to get her mother to let go, toddling over to Aunt Teresa in tears.

"Millie!" Anika started to lean forward, but Millicent was quickly back on her feet. If looks could kill, I figured I'd be dead twenty-times over.

"Y-you tripped me!" She yowled, jabbing a finger in my face. "I'll—I'll report you to immigrations! My husband is the chief of staff there. He'll have you thrown on the next bus to Mexico!"

"Jesus, *Millie!*" Aunt Teresa's face was screwed up in horror as she scooped Emily up into her arms. At this point, *everyone* was looking in our direction, uncomfortable grimaces plain on their face. A few covered their kids' ears, others quickly pushing them as far away from this crazy cow as possible. It wasn't that I wasn't used to this sort of thing, but the *extreme* reaction she had took me off-guard. I didn't really know how to respond to her; I just sat there, staring at her accusative finger.

Millicent must've noticed all the negative attention, because her voice dropped to a shaking whisper. "It-it's not fair. This is *my* special day—you have no idea how hard my life is right now."

That was the straw that broke Anika's back. She gently picked Bernadette up and off her lap, but before Millicent could try and grab her kid back from Aunt Teresa, Anika began pulling the slip down her legs, exposing her fairly provocative suit bottoms underneath. "Yeah, I bet your life's just *awful*," She began completely ignoring the puckered expression Millicent's face. "You live in an amazing neighborhood, with plenty of kids Emily's age to play with, and are just *so* inconvenienced by the three parked cars in your driveway. Must be terrible, having the freedom and cash to take yourself and your child anywhere you want."

"Anika," I reached out to touch her shoulder, but she pushed me away, fully engrossed in her rage.

"I bet it's *so* hard to have a loving husband, too!" Anika's voice only got louder and louder as she stepped toward Millicent, who, in turn, started shrinking away. "Someone who genuinely loves your truly terrible personality, who didn't marry you because he thought you had some hidden inheritance from your dead mother!"

All eyes went wide, including mine. There it was, all out on the floor for everyone to see. The big question that had been buzzing around my head since I met Anika; the reason for her divorce.

"Because, really, that's all I'm good for, right? Just, just cow-tailing to others who think they're better than me, *deserve* something from me." Anika was practically snarling now, having backed Millicent up against the desserts table. "You don't deserve a damn thing from me, *Millicent*. Not my time, not my lap, and *certainly* not Rashmi's patience." With a curt nod, Anika turned on her heel and marched back to our picnic table, leaving Millicent a quivering mess. "Come on, Bernadette. We're leaving."

Bernadette looked like her world had been completely shattered. Her hands were balling up the hem of her dress, but she quickly took her place by Anika's side. It only occurred to me now that she'd just watched her mom, essentially, change out of a swimsuit. The illusion had been broken; she was in silent tears.

"Anika, I can't even start," Aunt Teresa began.

Anika held up her hand. "You're not in control of what comes out of your sister's mouth. Hopefully, we can meet sometime for coffee. Just the two of us."

Aunt Teresa nodded, excusing herself from our little group as she carried off a still-crying Emily. "I'll still pay you," she quickly mentioned to me. "And a little extra. Seriously, I'm so sorry for all of this."

All I could do was nod back.

Chapter Nine

I'd never changed so quickly in my life. Anika were in and out of our suits in seconds, now standing on Millicent's front lawn to wait for the taxi Aunt Teresa had called (and had the foresight to offer paying for). Bernadette was welcome to play with the other kids while we waited, though Aunt Teresa swore up and down that Millicent would get *nowhere* near her. It left a heavy weight between Anika and I, something that had begun brewing the moment we stepped out of that house. She wanted to say something, I could feel it in my gut. But, given what happened when I asked the *last* person to tell me what it was, I was a bit hesitant to dive in.

"What a completely, despicable human being." Anika began. Her voice was cold, devoid of that usual spark of joy I'd grown used to.

I didn't respond to her. I wasn't sure if that's what she wanted.

"And-and the way she talked to you!" Anika huffed, arms crossing over her chest as a scowl cut its way across her face. "She was a real piece of work in high school, don't get me wrong, but this?" Anika scoffed. "This is a new low, even for her."

"She really upset you that badly?" I asked.

Anika looked at me like I'd just grown a second head. "How did she not upset *you* at all?"

"It's not that she didn't," I began. "I guess I just don't let it get to me personally."

Anika's brow rose. "She literally threatened to deport you."

"She'd have a rough time doing that, given how my family's Indian and not Mexican." I said jokingly.

That only seem to set Anika off more. "Rashmi, how can you be so calm about this? She treated you like the dirt on her lawn—she treated *us* like we were just props!"

"Well, that happens sometimes," I said. "Some folks just poke you for attention. You can't give it to them if you wanna get paid."

"So you rather I just let her push Bernadette off my lap?" Anika hissed. "Just so you could get *paid?*"

I could feel her eyes boring into my head, like she was daring me to agree. "N-No! I'm just saying that you might've made it a bigger deal than it was."

"Me?!" Anika's voice jumped an octave as she gave me an incredulous look. "Are you actually *chiding* me for standing up for myself? For standing up for you?"

"I didn't ask you to." Now the irritation was clear in my voice; what was with everyone assuming they knew what I wanted. First Hank, now Anika? "I'm not some porcelain doll that needs protecting."

Anika threw her hands up in the air, hair quickly undoing itself from the bun she'd attempted for the party. "Oh my God, I didn't say that!" It was the first time I heard her say, 'God' instead of some G-variant; it took me off-guard. "Why are you getting so up-in-arms about this? I didn't do anything wrong! I wasn't the one who cancelled plans last minute—" She suddenly stopped, eyes widening at her mistake.

Then she *was* upset about Pasta Night. "You said you were fine bringing pizza," I said slowly. "You agreed to compromise."

Anika nodded, still seething. "I did. But if I'm being honest, I didn't like it."

"Then why'd you agree to it?" I snapped. "We could've just rescheduled it!"

"*You* could've just kept your word and not planned on top of us!" Anika shouted back. "Bernadette was really looking forward to it—*I* was really looking forward to it—and you just tossed it aside like it was no big deal. And you picked *that* place, of all places," A visible shudder ran through her body. "It was like seeing my mother's ghost. It wasn't pleasant."

"You could've *said* something,"

"And what? Forced you to do something you *clearly* didn't want to?" Now Anika was shaking, tears springing from her eyes. It was like watching a Coke bottle overflow, one that had been shook too-many times. "I didn't *ask* for this. Bernadette doesn't deserve this. There's so much already going on in her life, and I swear, I'm not going to let a complete *stranger* add onto it."

That hurt a lot more than I expected. I could feel the tears pricking at the corner of my eyes as Anika stood across from me, unmoving, unsympathetic. This was an entirely new side to her, compiled from a mountain of struggles she'd dealt with up until this moment. I didn't know what to say. I didn't even know if I could *speak,* given the large lump growing in my throat.

"You don't mean that." I managed to croak out."

For a brief moment, Anika's expression softened. "No. And that's what makes this worse."

The taxi pulled up to the side of the driveway, giving a few honks to indicate their arrival. Anika started back to the house, going to collect Bernadette. I tried following after, but she spun around and stared me down. "Get your own ride home, Rashmi. I don't think it would be wise for use to sit in the same seat right now."

"What about Bernadette?" I flinched at the scathing look Anika gave me after uttering her daughter's name.

"I'll tell her you're busy. It wouldn't be new to her." With that, Anika turned, leaving me alone of the front lawn to grieve.

***

This had to be a new record for me. Somehow, in less than a week, I'd managed to piss off the two closest people to me. Walking out of that neighborhood was exhausting, but not because it was a good couple miles away from the apartment. My heart had never felt so heavy before, dragging alongside my feet as I numbly shuffled across crosswalks and streetways. How'd this even happen? It was all so quick, fueled by emotions until finally sputtering and crashing into a mess of hurt feelings.

"This is why I have cats." I half-heartedly mumbled under my breath.

After what felt like an eternity, I'd managed to make it back into the shopping district. A familiar ice-cream parlor caught my attention; Hank would be off today, and boy, did I need to drown my sorrow in something. With a heavy sigh, I pushed through the doorway, certain I had just enough in my pockets for my usual.

The place was surprisingly packed today. Almost every table had been taken, filled with families and teens alike. Evidently, the harrowing tale of the employee who stopped a kidnapping brought curious eyes to this place, much to the chagrin of the girl

118

behind the counter. She looked like a new hire, not just because I myself knew the names and faces of everyone who worked here, but because she looked completely out of her depth. Her uniform was crisp and new, somewhat ill-fitting around her chest as her hair slowly unraveled from her ponytail. She looked like a deer in headlights, trying to keep track of everyone's order. I hung back to watch the show for a bit; it was admittedly cathartic to know I wasn't the only one having a bad day.

Finally, the line thinned out, giving me my opening. As I approached, the poor girl looked ready to burst into tears. "H-Hi there. How can I...can I..." Her sentence was broken up by hiccupping sobs; I honestly felt bad for her.

"Hey, it's okay," I tried to reassure her. "First day on the job?"

She nodded, snot dripping from her nose.

"Well, you must have someone in the back showing you the ropes," I said. "I'm a usual, so they'll know my order right off the bat. Why not go grab them? You went through a *ton* of people just now."

The idea seemed revolutionary to her. With another nod, the girl nearly tripped over herself as she ducked into the back, obviously relieved to be out of the spotlight. I started drumming my fingers along the countertop, suddenly incredibly tired. Maybe I'd just take something to go, curl up in my apartment, and cry myself to sleep. It honestly seemed like the ideal way to spend the rest of this miserable evening.

"Hey, there."

My head immediately snapped up at the familiar voice. Standing behind the counter was Hank, looking just as surprised to see me as I did him. There wasn't any malice in his eyes, though, no sign of residual anger or distaste toward me. If anything, he looked as worn out as I did.

"H-hey." I glanced around, not entirely comfortable with looking in his eyes just yet. "Um, don't you have the day off?"

Hank jabbed his thumb behind him. "Boss asked me to help out the newbie today. Figured I could make a few extra bucks."

Silence hung between us.

Finally, I spoke, voice wobbling. "Um…w-well, you got a break coming up? It'll be my treat."

Hank was quiet for a moment, face carefully neutral. But, after a moment, a smile I hadn't seen in three days appeared. "I'm lactose-intolerant, you inconsiderate shit."

I broke out in laughter—a loud, somewhat hysterical, tearful sound—but a laugh nevertheless. "Like you've never suffered before for the stuff."

"You speak truth." Hank shrugged, untying his apron as he folded it neatly on top of the counter. "Let's take this for a walk. I've been stuck here for hours."

"What about…?" I glanced behind him at the double doors."

"What, Megan?" Hank followed my gaze, shaking his head. "Yeah…she'll be fine. Or I'll come back to this place on fire. Either way," He turned back to me, grinning. "It's a win-win in my book."

***

We had so much to catch up on. Enough that a quick walk around the block turned into a full jaunt to the park. I'd picked a bench for us to plop down on, an ideal location to both people-watch and chat without being overheard. Feeling like the center of attention, I insisted Hank spilled hits guts out first and he did so with gusto. In fact, he'd only now stopped to take a breath as we sat down.

"So, yeah," He said, arms hanging over the back of the bench. "I'm

pretty sure that new girl you saw is supposed to be my replacement."

I spooned some soupy ice-cream out of my cup but paused in mid-bite at the news. "Aw, Hank, that sucks. He seriously isn't going to keep his star child?"

Hank shrugged. "I thought he'd appreciate all the business, but apparently, keeping me around will just invite more hoodlums to try and jump the place."

"That's the most ass-backwards thinking I've ever heard."

Hank laughed, leaning over to snag my bite before I got the spoon to my lips. He shuddered from the sudden burst of cold, swallowing the mixture quickly. "You have the worst taste in ice cream."

"That's cause you don't like coffee, either." I said.

"You got me there." His expression shifted to something a bit more somber. "But, honestly? I'm not too torn up about getting canned. You were right, to some degree. I've sorta been living vicariously through you, and after seeing you brush with success..." He shrugged again. "I dunno. I lashed out a bit."

I stirred my ice cream, nodding. "Yeah, well, I wasn't in the right, either."

"I know," Hank stuck out his tongue playfully. "It takes two to tango, after all, even if you've got two left feet."

God, I missed his stupid face and that stupid wit of his. "So, what's the new plan, then? You know you're always welcome at my place, if yours gets too expensive."

"Might take you up on that offer," Hank chuckled. "If you'll have another animal in your house. Plus, I don't have the cutest neighbors in the whole world." He must've noticed my downtrodden expression, because he quickly added, "I mean, if that's something you still want. No pressure from this side, only support for your choices."

I let out a heavy sigh, abandoning my ice cream to the side as I slumped against the bench. "I don't think it's a choice I can make, anymore."

"Whaddaya mean?"

The tears were back in my eyes. One of the parlor's napkins was placed on my stomach, Hank's attention fully on me. "Thanks." I brushed it across my face, completely forgetting that I hadn't taken up my stage make-up. That was gonna look ugly in a hot second. "We had a fight. A big one; I don't know if Anika's gonna wanna see me again. There's so much of her I haven't seen, and I just pushed every single one of her buttons."

Hank gave me a sympathetic smile. "I mean, that's expected. But we had a fight, and we made up."

"I *really* messed up, though." I could barely speak without hiccup-sobs interrupting. "All she did was stand up for herself, stand up for me, against some lemon-faced bitch."

"Aw, I missed that?" Hank looked genuinely disappointed. "I woulda chewed her out for the both of you. What'd she say, anyway?"

For some reason, I started to giggle. "She threatened to deport me. To Mexico."

Hank dramatically inhaled. "Wow. She didn't even get the country right."

"And I got mad at Anika for calling her out on her BS." I sat up just enough to bend over, holding my head in my hands as they grew wetter by the second. "Why'd I *do* that? Anika didn't do anything *wrong*, and I just made myself look like a total clown."

"Hey, hey," Hank pulled me into a tight hug—I hadn't even realized I started hyperventilating. "Deep breaths, come on now..."

I hadn't realized how much I missed him until this moment. To have someone hold me while the world fell apart was something I *didn't* want to do alone. Is this what Anika was going through, was *still* going through. I couldn't even imagine lasting a few days, and she'd been going through likely *months* of it thanks to the divorce.

"Sh-she was so upset over Pasta Night," I managed to choke out. "You were r-right; I shouldn't have ever let my p-passion get in the way."

Hank pulled just enough away to wipe my face with his sleeve. "No, I didn't mean that. Rashmi, I can count on one hand the number of people who have been as lucky as you have," He swallowed loudly, looking ready to cry himself. "It's really inspirational. I can say with certainty now that I was jealous over it."

"Hank," I half-laughed, half-sobbed. "You're so lucky to have your dream take off like this *and* have someone you love."

That was a word I hadn't applied to myself and Anika, yet. Sure, I liked her plenty—every waking moment was spent trying to determine if she even wanted to go *out* with me—but love? Was it possible, and so quickly?

"I don't wanna lose her." My voice was barely a whisper. "Bernadette, Anika—I don't wanna lose either of them. But I don't want to give up on my dream, either."

Hank nodded, offering another wad of napkins my way. "Then we'll work on squishing it all together into one, new dream. Deal?"

I took the wad, finally able to smile for real. Before I could agree, though, my phone went off in the side of my backpack. Hank shot me a wide-eyed look. I did the same.

"Girl, answer it." He said.

I slung my pack off and reached for it, but hesitated. What if it was Anika? I couldn't handle another verbal chewing-out, even if I felt like I deserved one.

"Rashmi!" Hank snapped. "Would you answer the phone before I explode?"

I turned the screen upright, a mixture of relief and disappointment. "Unknown number," I said, turning to face it to Hank.

"Gimme." He snatched it up before I could object. "I feel like screwing with some telemarketers right now." Without hesitation, Hank pressed the TALK button, bringing the phone to his ear as he readied himself. "Hello?"

A pause. Then, the muffled voice spoke on the other side.

"No, this is Hank Esterbelt." Hank held the phone away from him, visibly confused. "Rashmi, who the hell is Teresa?"

My heart skipped a beat. "Put it on speaker, put it on speaker!"

Hank obliged as I quickly took over. "Teresa? This is Rashmi—Pearlglade?"

Another pause. Then, *"Oh, thank God. I was really hoping I could catch you, Rashmi."*

Hank shot me a raised eyebrow. I waved him away, fully focused on the conversation now. "Is something wrong, Miss Teresa?"

"Just 'Teresa' is fine." She said. *"I just wanted to make sure you were okay. I sincerely cannot apologize enough for what my sister said to you, or how she treated Anika."* I could hear her grimace. *"I know I shouldn't have, but, you and Anika were getting pretty loud out there. I hope you weren't fighting because of what Millie had done."*

"No, it's," I sighed, not wanting to bring Teresa further into this mess of a web. "It wasn't because of you."

"I really do feel awful," Teresa continued. *"If there's anything I can do—anything at all."*

"Can you hold that thought for a second?" Hank suddenly interjected.

"Oh. I mean, I suppose, but...

Hank immediately flipped the speakerphone off, muting the call as he stared at me. "You can't possibly know all these crazy-famous people."

"What are you talking about?" I asked.

Hank shook his head in disbelief, turn the mute off and speakerphone back one. "Hi, Hank again. Just curious; I'm not talking to *the* Teresa Sklar, am I?"

"Um, yes, that's my last name."

"As in the Teresa Sklar who owns all those big, fancy aquariums all across the U.S?"

My jaw dropped open. *That's* who that was?! "Hank how the hell did you,"

He waved a hand, pulling the phone closer to his face. "Miss Sklar—or, you prefer Teresa, right? My client holds absolutely no ill-will toward your family for the, ahem incident. I'm wondering, however, if we could talk business between us."

"I'm sorry, who are you, again?"

"Hank Esterbelt. I'm Rashmi's manager." He gave me a wink, but I was honestly still reeling over the number of incredibly wealthy and influential people I'd met in less than a month.

"Hank, what are you doing?" I hissed.

Again, he waved me off. "Well, Teresa, I'm incredibly grateful you decided to call us. While, as I mentioned, we certainly don't hold any ill-will against you personally, there is still the matter of damages themselves. Specifically, a loss in hours and the mental disturbance caused."

"Of course—I already promised to pay for the entire time, plus extra."

"And that's very kind of you to offer," Hank said. "But I would like to present a counteroffer, if you're interested.

"*Well,*" Teresa sounded hesitant. "*I certainly can try my best. What is it you're suggesting?*"

"Hank, I don't mind being paid more," I began.

Again, he shot me a look. "Excuse me for just a second, Teresa." Speakerphone off, mute turned on. "You wanna patch things up with the Jenners, right?"

"Well, sure, but how's an aquarium gonna fix that?" I asked.

A devilish grin crossed Hank's face. "You just leave that to me. I might've just found my calling."

Chapter Ten

This is *exactly* the sort of hair-brained scheme Hank would cook up. It wasn't a bad idea; with his newly discovered haggling prowess, he'd managed to snag three free tickets to the city aquarium (a trade-off for my extra pay, which I was only a touch disappointed about). Hank then made it seem like Teresa had given Anika and Bernadette the tickets as an apology, inviting them on a seemingly innocuous Saturday to come and have fun. She even offered to bring Emily along, just so Anika could have a bit of a break from watching her daughter and genuinely enjoy the trip.

Of course, nobody told them Pearlglade was going to be there, too.

I had been set up for hours ahead of time, dressed in my signature garb and placed on a jutting rock just above the touching tide pool. I had the usual employees to watch the critters and creeping hands, but my job was to sit and wave to the passersby. I got a ton of buzz, kids excitedly pointing and loudly giggling at their parents. Hank had even swung it to pay me for my time, though it wouldn't be as much as the actual swimmers got.

I'd take the cut for the sake of this plan actually working.

Hank suddenly appeared around the bend, out-of-breath and somewhat panicked. "Okay, okay, they're on their way over here. You ready?"

I so-totally wasn't. "Uh-huh."

Hank gave me a thumbs up, quickly pulling out his phone and pushing the speed dial. "They're almost here, Teresa. You got the music ready?"

"Yup, and the curtain's on standby." There was no way Teresa could hide her excitement. *"I think this is just so wonderful! Like something straight out of the movies."*

"Hopefully, this isn't supposed to be a satire." I grimaced.

"You're gonna do great," Hank reassured.

"I can't even *sing* that well, Hank!" I watched as the employees started pulling down on the sheer-fabric, magenta curtain, set up the night before on a circular hanger. "Why'd you say I could?"

"What proper mermaid doesn't sing?" Hank asked. "Besides, it's way more honest than just saying how you feel."

"And embarrassing," I added.

"And that's the point."

His phone crackled in his hand. *"All right, you two! She's on her way."*

"Places, everyone!" Hank skipped off into the crowd, quickly informing the crowd of the impending disaster that was about to happen. I was having major reconsiderations, but folks were already sitting around the tide pool, curious to see what was happening.

And then she appeared.

Anika rounded the corner first, dressed in a simple sundress with her hair pulled up into a loose ponytail. She found the crowd first, obviously confused, then she saw me. Teresa and Emily appeared next, though they quickly darted away as Anika put two and two together. We held an uncomfortable gaze, neither willing to break first. I wanted to show her that I knew I'd messed up, but I wasn't running. She couldn't scare me off, no matter what the baggage was.

"Mimi!" Bernadette seemingly appeared out of nowhere, making a mad dash across the aquarium to try and reach me. Hank quickly intercepted, kneeling down to quickly explain the plan in a hushed tone. Bernadette's face flipped from disappointed, to interested, to a full-out grin. She skipped over to the tide pool, leaning across just enough so I could hear her whisper. "You gonna make Mommy feel better?"

"I'm...gonna try." I said.

Bernadette nodded. "She's really sad, you know."

"I know."

"She misses you a lot." Bernadette reached her hand out toward mine; I took it. "I do, too. Are we gonna play again, soon?"

I looked up at Anika, who'd taken to leaning against the wall way off to the side. Still, she was in view of the tide pool. She was waiting to see what I'd do.

"Yeah. We will, Bernie."

That seemed to satisfy her, at least for now. With that, Bernadette hurried back to her mother's side; it was me against the growing crowd, isolated on my little island and draped in my shimmering curtain. My stomach was doing backflips, every butterfly in the world seemingly crammed inside and going crazy. But as the music started playing behind me on the speakers, I knew it was too late.

It was sink or swim time.

I hadn't been lying, either. My singing voice was on par with a howling cocker spaniel. I started out rocky, having to clear my throat a few times as I tried picking back up on the melody. A few folks gave me a reassuring cheer, and soon, I started to get into the groove. The song had been written between Hank and myself, a collection of my thoughts and feelings currently being announced to the rest of the world.

It was a song about the time I spend with the Jenners, the first time we met, all the emotions that ran through my head whenever we were together, whenever we were apart, all under the clever guise of a mermaid who'd been stranded out in the dark, lonely sea. How she'd met a mother and daughter on a similarly-drifting ship, how they let her on and had so much fun together. How that ship wasn't in the best of shape—there were patched-up holes, barnacles on the underside, even some damage left behind by the mermaid—but it was somewhere the mermaid wanted to stay. And, if she could stay, I would work to help fix it right alongside that mother and daughter sailing pair.

Suddenly, the music faded out. It was over. I didn't know when I'd closed my eyes, but as I opened them, I was greeted by a thunderous round of applause. Regardless how terrible I may or may not have sounded, the idea must've gotten across. I'd even gotten some of the sappier adults to tear up.

That included Anika, who was still standing off in the back. Clapping along with everyone else.

Smiling.

***

Even though I hadn't *touched* water, I still had to go shower off in the employee's lounge. It was just protocol, but part of me wanted to get out as fast as possible and go talk somewhere private with Anika. She'd given me the slightest hope with that smile of hers and I didn't want to waste it. So I did my best to work the shower's handles, hissing and letting out tiny, surprised shrieks as the water flipped from ice-cold to scalding hot. Finally, I'd found a comfortable-enough temperature to slide underneath and begin quickly washing off the imaginary, aquarium water.

And then Anika's voice called out from inside the lounge area.

I turned the water off, poking my head out from the curtains. I'd heard her, right? It could've just been the pipes, my imagination kicking into overtime after that adrenaline-filled performance.

"Uh, Rashmi? Teresa said you were back here...?"

Nope. That was definitely her. "I'm back here, Anika. Gimme a sec to towel off."

"Ah, d-don't bother!" The door to the shower room swung open as Anika entered, looking a lot more soaked than she did before. "Teresa said I could, um, come back and clean up."

I bit back a snort. "What happened?"

"Bernadette got a little excited over holding one of the crabs." That's all Anika was willing to share as she began to pull the dress over her head.

"Uh," My heart nearly jumped out my mouth as I quickly shut the curtains. "D-D-Do you want me to leave?"

I could hear Anika scoff from behind the curtains. "Oh, please. You've seen me in a bathing suit, how's my underwear any different?"

She had me there. "I mean, I guess they're the same."

"Glad we can agree." My curtain was suddenly pulled aside as Anika stepped in. The space wasn't exactly built for two people; our bodies pressed up against each other as she pulled the curtain shut. I'd seen her in a suit, but this *was not the same*. She wore a matching pair of laced-green garments, hair neatly shaved in all the right places while milky-white breasts were secured properly in place, dotted all across in freckles. I worked my way up to her face; she patiently waited.

"Why," I began to ask.

"I figured neither one of us could run away this time." Anika's expression shifted, as if that was a point against her. "It's…safe to say you're the one who put this all together for us?"

I nodded dumbly, unable to ignore as her perky chest brushed up against mine. "I-I mean, I had help."

Anika nodded, her hands folding gently across her stomach. We were quiet for a moment, letting the trickling of shower water fill the voice as both literal and figurative steam drifted between us.

"Have you ever sang in public before?" Anika suddenly asked.

I shrugged. "N-Not really. Was it that bad?"

"It was…rough." Anika said. "But heartfelt. Anyone watching could see that."

Another bout of silence.

"Anika," I was ready to spill my heart out on the ground before. Apologize for the fight, tell her how every word of that song was the truth and I felt such inexplicable things for. How much I missed seeing Bernadette, how much I wanted us to be together, even if I myself was a total mess. I wanted to share in her anxiety, her darkest days; it would all be worth it, just to say I was with her.

But before I could do any of that, Anika kissed me.

She'd lifted herself onto the tips of her toes, the warm water running down our cheeks as her lips pressed against mine. It was startling at first, feeling her tongue explore every inch of my mouth. Her arms hung gently around my neck, never forcing the encounter on me. Not that she even had to ask twice; my tongue began playing with hers as I leaned in, my hands securing around her waist.

Anika took me in completely, nipples perked and rubbing against my chest as she broke free for a moment, gasping. Her lips continued down my neck, each newly discovered sweet-spot pulling a gentle moan deep from my throat. My fingers worked their way up her back, feeling through each curl in her hair, every knot and beautiful tangle on that head of hers. "A-Anika,"

A rush of water splashed against my back, sending rolling shudders down my spine as she rose back up to catch my lips. Her intention was obvious; this wasn't a time for words. Just like I had, she wanted to express herself through something far more personal. We slowly sank to the ground, legs interwoven while the tips flexed, tightening and relaxing with each new discovery. Every drop of water was amplified now; ever touch, every kiss, a euphoric tingle a top my skin. Anika's fingers were like silk, barely touching my collarbone, yet still managing to light up my insides.

"I'm sorry," she moaned, her head lifting to brush her lips across my forehead. "This is so…I'm sorry…"

I cut her off this time, breathing in her apology with another kiss on the lips. Our hands met on my stomach, gently gliding across the glistening skin while we shuddered together. "I want to be with you." I said breathlessly. "Every part of you, since the day we met."

Anika slid her body on top of mine, head rested in the crook of my breast as she continued exploring my lower abdomen. "I'm so broken," she said. "There's so many pieces, everywhere.

I gasped gently, a warmth spreading up through my body. "I-I'm not perfect, either."

She choked out a giggling-sob. "Can we be not-perfect t-together, then?"

I wanted nothing else but that. In a perfect world, this coital moment would last forever. Just our bodies, together, lost in this heavy, hot steam. "We m-might not want to continue this in a public shower," I managed to stammer out."

That quickly killed the mood. "O-Oh, no," Anika went to sit up, only to slid and smack right into my stomach. I let out a gasping wheeze, all the air knocked completely out of my lungs. "Ah, R-Rashmi--!" Her face portrayed concern, but she had fully dissolved into laughter. "I'm s-so sorry."

I gave her a thumb's up, still fighting to gather air for a number of reasons.

"Y-You're right, though. I didn't think about how gross," This time, Anika kept her balance by grabbing onto the shower knob. "Oh, gosh, this really *is* gross. I just thought it would be s-spontaneous, but," She was still giggling, trying her best to control herself.

Not that I was any better. I sat up, stomach spasming from my own chuckle-fit. "N-no, it was," I couldn't even finish, so I opted to stand and catch Anika in a surprise kiss.

"Is this going to b-be our go-to when we have no words?" She asked as we pulled away.

"Would it be so bad if it was?" I asked.

It was the first time I saw a spark of mischief behind Anika's smile. "No. I suppose it wouldn't."

Epilogue

This had been the day all of us had been dreading. Anika and I stood on the steps of the courthouse, its looming shape an awful visage on such a nice, summer day. It'd been coming for months now, but even as the calendar continued to shrink, I still couldn't believe it was here.

The last custody hearing over Bernadette.

I held Anika's hand in mind, carefully observing her features. She was deceptively calm, a neutral frown on her face as she stared the building down. It was like watching someone try to win a staring contest with a cat.

I gave her a quick kiss on her cheek. Her stony exterior broke.

"Rashmi--!" A fit of giggles spilled out as the life came back into her eyes. "Come on, I was trying to get ready."

"What, don't want Douglas to see you the happiest you've ever been?" I asked.

"Bold assumptions on your part," Anika grinned, planting a tiny kiss on my nose as I scrunched into a frown. "But I want the judge to take me seriously."

"We've got this," I gave her hand a reassuring squeeze. "We look like stellar parents on paper! Our own condo in the kid-friendliest neighborhood, two very lucrative jobs."

"Which he might not see as credible work," Anika mumbled under her breath.

"And to that, we just flip our figures and fingers." I said.

Again, Anika snickered. "Not that last part, though. Douglas' lawyer is going to pull every trick to try and make us look bad."

"Ooh, I hope he tries for the 'lesbian' card." I grinned. "Nothing sings credibility like claiming we're turning Bernadette into one of the gays."

Anika waved me off, expression losing its radiant touch. "You think we've got this, then? Be honest."

I took a deep breath, softening my smile so she knew I was serious. "Yeah. I really think we do."

Anika nodded, turning once more to face the courthouse. "Okay. Well, let's go, then."

"Oh, wait!" I fished around my bag for a moment, producing two, colorful scarves. "Hank insists we wear these."

Anika gave me a bemused grin but accepted the scarf. They were both a pink and teal ombre, a flash of stars scattered here and there as two mermaid silhouettes swam across. "Is this his newest design?"

"Yeah. Teresa said they'll be in her gift shops within the week." Never knew the guy had a talent for sewing, but damn, did this look professionally made. "The colors were picked specially for us."

"I wonder where he got the idea?" Anika grinned.

I quickly wrapped the scarf around my head, doing a quick turn to show it off. "How do I look?"

"Like a small child wrapped a towel around there head. Here," she undid my messy knots and motioned me to knee down. "You really wanna hid your hair? I think it's growing in nicely!"

I gave her a scoff. My hair was a weird, stuck-up mess, the follicles not used to be any longer than a millimeter. "Hell no. Besides, wearing it like this gives it the *magical* properties."

Anika laughed as she secured the scarf in place. "Is that a story I need to hear later?"

"I dunno." I stood, catching my arms around her waist as I pulled her close. "You gotta be a big kid to hear it."

"Mmm." Anika grinned, her nose gently brushing against mine. "I'm pretty mature for my age. I could show you later this evening."

"Bernadette."

"Is with Aunt Teresa and Uncle Hank tonight." The way Anika batted her eyelashes made me wanna go home there and then. "We have the house all to ourselves."

"Then let's get this over with." I pulled away just enough so my arm was still around her waist. "You ready, Sea Lily?"

Anika secured her hand around my waist as well. "Of course, Pearlglade."

With that, we mounted the stairs together, determined to take on whatever was waiting for us behind those double-doors.